Praise for *House on the River*

"We see an imaginary hand reach out from Rapoport's talent to try to grab a feeling that shimmers, just beyond reach as we get older. The river, long afternoons, the dock, a book. Summer."
　　　　　　　　　　　　　　　　　　—SUSAN SALTER REYNOLDS,
Los Angeles Times Book Review

"Nessa Rapoport writes like a poet, muses like a philosopher, and loves like the mother (and daughter and granddaughter) that she is. *House on the River* is about family but also much more. It is a startlingly original work, as intricate as a jewel and as vast as a library full of your favorite books."
　　　　　　—STEPHEN J. DUBNER, author of *Turbulent Souls* and
Confessions of a Hero-Worshiper

"I have never read such a luminous meditation on a private journey. Nessa Rapoport writes about her family in spare, vibrant, poetic prose. I am moved by the layers of meaning as they weave in and out like fine music. This is memoir as prayer."
　　　　　　—ELIZABETH SWADOS, composer and playwright of
Runaways and *Alice in Concert*

Praise for *Preparing for Sabbath*

BOOKS IN CANADA FIRST NOVEL AWARD SHORT-LIST

"The story of a young woman's quest to find both love and God . . . A novel by a talented new writer."

—*Los Angeles Times*

"Intense, emotional, often poetic, the book catches and holds the reader." —*Milwaukee Journal*

"The story of a young Jew's search for spiritual meaning has been written before, but not from a woman's point of view. An incisive, lyrical novel." —*Flare*

"A warm, wise novel suffused with the blue radiance of yearning."

—AMOS OZ, author of *A Tale of Love and Darkness*

EVENING

ALSO BY NESSA RAPOPORT

House on the River: A Summer Journey
A Woman's Book of Grieving
Preparing for Sabbath

The Schocken Book of Contemporary Jewish Fiction
(co-editor, with Ted Solotaroff)

COUNTERPOINT
BERKELEY, CALIFORNIA

nessa rapoport

EVENING

A novel

NESSA
RAPOPORT

Library of Congress Cataloging-in-Publication Data
Names: Rapoport, Nessa, author.
Title: Evening : a novel / Nessa Rapoport.
Description: First hardcover edition. | Berkeley, California :
Counterpoint Press, 2020.
Identifiers: LCCN 2020000291 | ISBN 9781640094086
(hardcover) | ISBN 9781640094093 (ebook)
Subjects: LCSH: Domestic fiction.
Classification: LCC PS3568.A627 E94 2020 | DDC 813/.54—dc23
LC record available at https://lccn.loc.gov/2020000291

Jacket design by Nicole Caputo
Book design by Wah-Ming Chang

COUNTERPOINT
2560 Ninth Street, Suite 318
Berkeley, CA 94710
www.counterpointpress.com

Printed in the United States of America

1 3 5 7 9 10 8 6 4 2

For Tobi and our children

For Lisa, Mimi, and Liz, *z"l*

And for all whose love sustained me and brought me to this day

FIRST
DAY

ONE

One loves, the other is loved: so Nana taught us. I look at the beautiful bones of her face and speculate about this pronouncement. My grandmother has always been beloved, and so my grandfather, long dead, assumes a peculiar poignancy. Once, in some rapturous, unimaginable youth before she married, Nana was the ardent lover. But no one is alive to tell us about the object of her affection, and she will not disclose his name.

We are sitting in the living room of my mother's house, waiting for the funeral to begin. Outside, the sky is the eerie pewter I remember from my childhood, lightless even at midday. In this room six years ago, before our mother recovered the furniture yet again, Tam and I were laughing at the weather. Then, too, it was noon when I realized, after her baby's naming ceremony was over and the last guests had straggled out, that the day would not improve, that, to quote Tam: "This is it."

I had fled to New York, whose winters are tamed by the city's determination to outwit the season. Tam not only stayed in Toronto, betraying our pact to leave the minute we could, but chose a profession that forced her to rise most mornings at four in order to be on the air. For her, the half year of darkness is permanent, I think to myself. And then think: Permanent darkness.

Paralyzed, I stare at Nana, imploring her to rescue me, but she is stoic, not emitting whatever feelings she no doubt has. The fact is, my sister, her eldest grandchild, is dead. The silence in this room is not the anticipatory hush preceding a family celebration but the void of what cannot be accommodated.

"Tam."

In speaking my sister's name, I have invaded Nana's solitude. I look at her carefully and observe, even in the somber room, that the skin beneath her eyes is gleaming. No one has seen my grandmother cry.

"Laurence is coming," I state, more bluntly than intended.

Nana's lips draw into a pucker of distaste. Once again Eve has said the wrong thing. Why doesn't my admiration of my grandmother offset her reservations about me? One reason might be that as soon as I utter Laurie's name, my body ignites, despite the house's chill, despite the fact that it has been years since I lay naked on my grandmother's bed at the cottage, tonguing Laurie from his kiss-bitten mouth to the taut circles of his bent knees.

"Typical." I hear Tam sniff. "I'm not even in the ground."

Whenever I come home, I fancy myself an outlaw. Years ago, one of Tam's friends asked me at a party, "Does your mother feel like a failure because you had to leave Toronto?"

"'Had to leave Toronto'?" I ranted to Tam afterward. "Does he really believe all human beings want to live four blocks from their parents so they can eat together every Sunday night at the Bagel King? I chose to live in New York, as any person with—"

"I know"—she said tolerantly—"a large soul."

"'Inviting thighs,' I was going to say."

"Oh, Eve," said Tam, predictably.

Then I smile, because she has been brought back to me. My grandmother turns away. She may not want to judge me but she cannot help herself. I, who secretly view myself as her true disciple, find that at thirty-five I am back in my usual role in our diminished family.

I concentrate on the dark green velvet that successfully masks the previous sofa while my mind considers when my father will arrive from his house; whether or not my mother will be collected enough to come downstairs; if Tam's children, in the new enlightenment, will be brought to the cemetery; and, the thought that closes my throat, what Tam looked like at her death.

I know her body as well as I do my own. Tam did not allow me into her room in these last weeks, to the separate anguish of my parents, who believed she was trying to spare her little sister. Despite their pleas, she stoutly maintained that for my sake I should not come, that we had chosen to speak only by phone. My mother reluctantly acquiesced. My father, in a conference call he imposed, negotiated with each of us in turn, but we were united and implacable.

When he gave up, it was with one of his favorite exhortations. "At least you girls get along. If I ever hear that the two of you are fighting, even after I'm dead—"

"—you'll turn over in your grave," Tam said.

Normally, in this abnormal situation, we would have giggled morbidly in the knowledge that she seemed headed for the grave a lot sooner than he did. But my father, holding forth, was not listening to himself. "Which would not be the first time," I could hear Tam say acerbically.

The worst of several burdens I am trying to ignore is

that Tam and I fought continuously since she got sick, as if the disease had afflicted our relationship along with her body, and that two weeks before she died we argued so vehemently we did not speak again. As children, we had a truce that the sister who leaves the house after a fight has to shout into the closing door, "I love you, I love you," in case she were killed in a car crash before mending the rift. Now I have committed the ultimate offense, whose consequences I must bear alone.

Do all people have one story that haunts them throughout their lives? Nana has told me hers so often I can recite it in her cadence. Unfortunately, the tale has a moral I provoke, not by any conscious act but by my face and manner. In a deferred legacy, I resemble her fabled sister Nell, source of Nana's unremitting grief and self-reproach. As I listened to Nana's words, I could not tell whether to be flattered by the attention or repelled by the analogy.

"Nell was the most beautiful girl," Nana would declare in wonderment. "You cannot imagine her loveliness. Pictures never did her justice; she had such a way about her."

I have dissected the snapshots of Nana's sister many times, looking for that beauty and carriage, but, like Zelda Fitzgerald's photographs, the extant few of Nell do not yield the mysterious allure that was the cause of so much suffering.

"She made trouble wherever she went," Nana said. "When our sister Abigail finally had a beau to call on her, Nell had only to toss her head and the boy never looked at Abby again. Of course, Nell tired of him in a week. The girl was born without a conscience."

At this point in the story I feel a familiar disquiet, leavened by my amusement at Nana's unselfconscious narration. "Pull up a plant to see its roots and kill the plant," she was wont to say if I pressed her to concede her intent. I am not unmindful of the fact that my grandmother is comparing me to an amoral tease.

"On my own wedding day, when I went to put on my silk stockings—" Nana opened the box to find them snagged and torn, borrowed by Nell without permission and brazenly returned.

I do not change the subject. Like someone afraid of heights who is drawn to stairwells and precipices, I am fascinated by Nana's version of her sister, whom I knew only as a skittery, defeated old woman with a nimbus of faded hair.

The hair is an indispensable part of the tale. Nell had

thick red hair, not the carroty red bemoaned by Anne of Green Gables, but mahogany curls with lights of copper that she styled in elaborate, varied arrangements—a more trivial example of her flair for life that should, according to Nana, have rendered her sister immune from life's blows rather than enticing them.

Nana's reverence for physical beauty can oddly humanize her magisterial intellect. More often, it is tiresome. Nana herself is beautiful, which she knows but will not allow. And I am no femme fatale luring men into disastrous entanglements. I would never betray my sister, either by ruining her clothes or stealing her beaux. Yet some part of me is thankful to be the reflection of my grandmother's obsession, however distorted and to my detriment. Nana's love is imperial and remote. At least I compel her interest.

Waiting for the doorbell to chime is like waiting for Canada to change. I have never been able to explain to my family why this country's most soothing feature, its sedate proceeding from one occurrence to the next, is such an irritant to me, inciting behavior more outrageous than I'd planned.

"Drama queen," says Tam inside my head.

Although I do make inconsistent attempts to deflect the way my family perceives me, on the morning of my sister's funeral even I am amazed at what I've wrought.

Over the years I have tried not to think about Laurie. Once, when I asked Tam if she ever ran into him, her verdict was definitive: "Boring and suburban."

But lately, each time I came home, I did enact one ritual. I sneaked into the den to look up his name in the phone book. The sight of his address—always the same—was equated in my mind with his reassuring constancy, a devotion I had forfeited by leaving the city as I did.

Yesterday, I saw that Laurie had moved. His wife's name was no longer beside his. When I read the new numbers next to his bare name and thought, "I'll ask Tam what happened to his marriage," I felt shaky. I should have called Simon in New York, as I had promised. Instead, I memorized Laurie's number.

Hearing his machine message, I intended to hang up. Then I announced myself and said starkly, "My sister is dead." I breathed so that I wouldn't cry, and put down the receiver.

At once I remembered the first long-distance call between Laurie and me. We had not spoken in a week—a lifetime at seventeen. Laurie and I had made an intricate plan, taking into account the time difference between Toronto

and Florence. But when the operator called on the anticipated day, the circuits were busy, once, twice, again.

My mother was nothing if not a romantic. Applying her
charms, she cajoled the operator into trying continually, on
behalf of starstruck lovers everywhere. When the operator
finally informed me my party was waiting, I was so over-
wrought I could not talk. Nothing seemed momentous
enough for the occasion.

I sat on my bed, atypically mute.

"This has to be the most expensive silence your mother
ever paid for," Laurie said.

Last night I stared at the phone, willing it to ring. Throughout the evening people called; I delivered the funeral arrangements mechanically. At midnight, in defiance of a code
I didn't know I lived by, I picked up the receiver and called
Laurie again.

"I thought it was too late," he said. He knew about Tam:
What could he do to help?

The timbre of his voice had an extraordinary effect. I entered an idyll of our lovemaking so tactile I could dispel it
only when he repeated my name.

Astonished, I invited him to come to the house before the funeral began, an idea unconventional enough for him to question it and then decide aloud that whatever might comfort me, the mourner, must be right to do.

Since I've come home my mind has been running frantically in and out of the past without transition. Nothing I think about seems to hold still long enough to catalogue it in its appropriate tense.

And so it has been more disconcerting than usual to return to my mother's house. Although I am under the roof beneath which Tam and I grew up, the decor reflects my mother's endless faith that physical transformation will produce a more profound change, as if interior design were a spiritual term. This conviction has sanctioned her to redo the living room with unsettling frequency. I can never be sure where I'll be when I walk in.

Several years ago, I had entered a subtle space of unbleached linen and dun-colored cotton, the summer house of an industrial magnate. At the start of Tam's illness, the room hardened to glass and metal. But on the morning of my sister's funeral, I find myself waiting for Laurie in an English sitting room, not unlike the parlors of Nana's youth.

Nana and I face each other on matching velvet sofas, accompanied by oversized cabbage-rose chairs. Braided tassels cinch the draperies, released onto the floor in moiré splendor.

Today, Laurie is the curiosity I have allotted myself. Nana used to like him, until she knew we were sleeping together. She grew up with his grandfather, children of the only two Jewish families to summer in their tiny Ontario town. The connection was all that protected me from her wrath.

Not that she and I, ever, said a word about sex. It was not proper form for a woman born in the reign of King Edward VII. We are ten years from the millennium, but Nana is unable to shed the post-Victorian constraints of her childhood.

The look on her face when she acknowledges that Laurie is on his way recalls instantly the silences that would descend upon Nana and me.

I want to tell her not to worry. I am braced for the nice man with an incipient paunch who will offer condolences to both of us. My ear is alert for the doorbell when Laurie appears, conjured, in the archway of the living room.

Laurie was a boy when I loved him, his youth an emblematic condition representing not only his chronological age but an essence, a nectar I could imbibe to counter my persistent sense of dislocation in this city. He was wholly of his place and era, belonging in Toronto, where he would inherit his father's business or go into law, as, in fact, he did;

marry someone from his neighborhood and live happily ever after, while I sought grandeur and danger in New York.

But when Laurie steps inside, "boring and suburban" are hardly the words that come to mind. Tam and I must have different taste in men, I think. My hands, folded decorously in my lap, are already tracing the planes of his face as if I were eighteen and still in love with him. My fingers are inside his mouth. His clothes fall away, and I see what he looks like naked.

I feel myself color at my imagination's transgression and lower my head. When I look up, I can read his face. He was never as articulate as I, and in my clairvoyance I know that he is struggling to say something to Nana and me, and that he is too full of feeling to say it.

When he clasps Nana's hand, a final surprise overtakes me. I begin to cry, mortifying myself and embarrassing my grandmother. Laurie moves away from her to me and lifts me up.

My body reads every muscle I intuited moments ago. Although my tears, unconnected to my volition, will not stop, I am alight with desire, not the easy flirtation I foresaw but the real thing, the encounter of memory and chemistry that happens rarely and seems irresistible.

Is he feeling it as well? In my experience, "vast," says Tam within, the body cannot lie. Laurie steps back as if scorched, and his voice, formal, discreet, inquires after my mother and my father, civility restored. But I know something is going to happen. And I hear Tam, confirming that I'm right.

◆

Since Tam's diagnosis, I have had a recurring dream, one I used to have as a child that my unconscious filed and then retrieved for this emergency.

I am in the bedroom of my grandmother's cottage, the one overlooking the lake. The room is softened by light; sky and water are a placid gray. The lake is lapping quietly at the narrow beach, encroaching so incrementally that at first I do not realize the beach has disappeared. Now the water is at the wooden back steps. Now the steps are hidden. The lake is rising, inexorable as it climbs the house, blind, remorseless, until the wall of water reaches the roof. From inside, all I see is the merging of gray lake and sky until the cottage is engulfed.

Sex is the only antidote to death that I've discovered, but even Simon's dexterous lovemaking in my apartment or his does not prevent the dream from coming back—memorably, twice in the same long night. Psychologists like to debate the question, Does insight lead to change? No insight would lead to the change I require: that Tam's decree be reversed, like a rented movie scurrying backward in order to be returned the next day, its plot already forgotten.

TWO

I AM STANDING AT THE GRAVESITE OF MY SISTER, dreaming of plums. The ripe, rose-colored ones with the blushing flesh within, the kind I would bite into greedily while Tam looked on, half appalled, half envious of my gluttony.

Beneath the soles of my boots, the unyielding cold of the ground punctures my summer reverie. For once, I have dressed like a grown-up, in a coat conservative enough for Tam's wardrobe. As a result, my teeth are chattering in an exaggerated fashion and I cannot feel my feet. I want to wrap my arms around myself, but Ella, Tam's daughter, is squeezing my gloved hand with insistent fingers.

Above, the sky has the blank look of imminent snow. I am enclosed by my family: My father in a stiff hat, towering over everyone; my mother at my side, crying so hard she does not know I'm here. Tam's husband, Ben, is composed, a rebuke. In from Vancouver, my uncle Gil leans on Nana, who is erect as a monarch on an old coin.

There are scores of people, many from Tam's television world, the adult life she created in Toronto. It is not tasteful to look around so avidly, but I do, despite the horror, the open rectangle before me.

I recognize some of Dad's partners, crimped with empathy. I haven't seen them in many years, but I know each face nonetheless, like a police illustration that heralds what someone who is missing will look like decades later. I can visualize the hall of offices on the way to my father's, the blue ribbon of Lake Ontario in his window. In my mind I am still a child, running soundlessly down the pale carpeting to surprise him.

Now he is here, stricken. One of the men in tweed overcoats who surround him must have closed his office door to sit with Tam while she reviewed her will. She never would have left this world without one.

What secrets is she taking with her, I find myself

wondering, as the dismayingly small box is lowered into the depths.

◆

Tam had a secret drawer when we were children. The skull-and-bones warning on its face taunted me from the day she proclaimed that the drawer was forbidden to anyone in the family.

One summer evening, I waited until the upstairs was empty and tiptoed into her sanctuary. Tam's curtains stirred faintly. Outside, my father was sliding the hose in a green arabesque across the lawn.

I dragged Tam's desk chair to the dresser, my heart clattering. When I pulled its glinting handle, the secret drawer made a plaintive sound.

Below me, my mother was making her own kitchen sounds. I hoped I had calibrated the friction in the house precisely, with my parents in their separate principalities. When I would hear their voices rise in the crescendo they could not dampen, I'd dream of being invisible. First, I would be Eve, and then I'd simply dissolve, transparent Eve-molecules surveying their former domain in unassailable tranquility.

The light was already dim, but I could not admit my presence by turning on the lamp. For a minute I hesitated, imagining all too easily the purgatory to which Tam would consign me if she found me posed at her dresser. Then, as usual, my passion to know everything prevailed.

Peering over the lip of the open drawer, I saw only two treasures, positioned perfectly like every other object in her room. A purple felt whiskey bag, its gold drawstring tight. And a locked diary, whose key was inexplicably beside it.

Unsurprisingly, the diary was the focus of my attention. Swiveling the tiny key to release the clasp, I eagerly turned the waxy, scented pages. What would I discover that would explain with finality not Tam's secrets but the secret of Tam, the fascination she held for me in her orderliness, her certainty about what she wanted, and the discipline she could so easily summon to get it.

But there were no confidences in these pages. Tam's diary read like an army manual: "Morning: Up: 6:45 a.m. Sit-ups: 10 min. Shower: 7 min. Dress: 3 min. Eat: 5 min. Brush teeth: 1.5 min. School. Home: English: 40 min. History: 35 min. Called Anne: 7 min. Susie called me: 9 min. Bed: 9:45. Anthology: 15 min."

I read every page, yawning with tedium and yet compelled. There was something ferocious, spellbinding, in her relentless transcription of the mundane.

Today's date had no writing. I fanned the future's pages. Blank. Blank.

And then, isolated in capital letters: "EVE."

I turned the page and squinted to read the lone sentence.

"I know something Eve doesn't know."

Even when I splayed the last pages, the diary held no clue to help me decode her tantalizing prelude. Tam had verbalized the operating assumption of our lives.

I yanked open the mouth of the whiskey bag. In seconds I was coughing spasmodically from soap dust. Tam seemed to have saved every bar of soap Daddy had brought us from the hotel rooms of his European trips. Now they were disintegrating in her secret drawer. I jammed the diary's clasp into the lock and shoved the drawer closed.

It was truly dark. My father must have come inside. I heard my mother's annoyed rejoinders, while outside the sprinkler began its consoling night music. Then Tam was calling me to supper. I would have to enter the dining room's abrupt light, guarding my own secret while all my feelings for her—devotion, guilt, and a confused yearning—lobbied me in competing percussion.

The first shovelful of earth knocks brutally on the wood of the coffin. My father has always set store by the uncompromising rituals of Jewish mourning. To participate in burial honors the dead. He straightens up and steps back from the edge.

I wish I could lift one of the shovels lying about for this purpose, move a single clot of earth from the raw mound to the grave, particularly when I see Nana wrestling with the metal handle, her white puffs of breath like an SOS in the crystalline air. No one tries to dissuade her.

Then Ella says, "Now, Daddy?" I look down to see her quite lyrically arch into the sky the rose Ben gives to her. Almost black, like a smudge of blood, it falls into the hole without a sound.

I bite my lip to prevent my whimpering. The wind has picked up, piercing my chest. The rims of my ears feel brittle. Arrhythmic thumps are having a strange effect inside my head. Now I know what people mean when they say the earth rushes up, I think idly. But I do not find out what fainting feels like, because Laurie grasps my arm, standing so firmly at my wilting side that I cannot fall.

The purity of the air has heightened my senses. I can smell Laurie's skin, feel through my coat the nubby texture of his. Beside my feet are embossed leather wingtips, neatly aligned.

When I knew Laurie, he wore cowboy boots, fringed suede vests, and silk shirts I couldn't wait to pull out of his jeans.

As the funeral ends, I remember the least predictable fact about him. Beneath the weathered denim, Laurie wore nothing.

The first time I undressed him, I had been more surprised by the immediacy of his nakedness than by the fact that my friendship with him seemed to have undergone spontaneous combustion. One moment he was Tam's younger buddy, exemplar of Toronto's provincial confidence. Then my startled face undid all the sophistication I'd affected to deter his interest. "Now look who's provincial," his bobbing penis seemed to say.

The boys I knew before Laurie wore white jockeys, and I would have bet money on Laurie as a white jockey guy.

"Eve!"

I jump. It is Tam, exasperated by my discursion at her funeral on men's underwear.

"I can't help it," I whisper back.

As if in divine affirmation, my eyes light on the tombstone ahead. There, in simple lettering, my great-aunt Nell's name is inscribed. I thought she was buried somewhere in Arizona, where she'd lived in old age, but the family must have decided to bring her home.

◆

Throughout my twenties, I traveled. While others traipsed from sight to sight in classic European cities, I could be found at a café table, my notes before me untouched as I waited in the sleepy square of an Iron Curtain town, sipping an iced drink, encircled by children hawking souvenirs, the dusty trees almost motionless. I frequented markets; I listened to women haggling over desiccated root vegetables.

Ostensibly, I was engaged in research, following in the footsteps of young British women who had set out at the end of the Great War to assess in writing the consequences of the catastrophe that had decimated a generation of fiancés, husbands, and brothers. Certainly I was becoming an expert on atmosphere.

Meanwhile, Tam's alarm clock was ringing before dawn. She washed her hair, ate in the car as she drove downtown, and took the elevator skyward to a production room where she worked without lunch until well after dark. Tam had been assured that if she persevered, she had the talent to be on the air.

Although Tam knew the chic places that had begun to spring up near her job, we met for our reunions at Fran's, the all-night dive of our high school years. There we would sit in the corner booth, drinking refills of coffee into which we poured one fluted container of cream after another.

Our brains lit up by caffeine, we played our parts. She ranked herself on the scale of her ambition. I relayed my adventures, with a soupçon of misgiving.

"My tombstone will declare, 'She had potential.'"

Tam restated her belief in me. "No," she said. "'Late bloomer.'"

Sitting in the coffee shop window, her face illuminated by the sporadic glare of the dwindling cars on St. Clair Avenue, she wistfully added, "When I die, mine will be inscribed: 'She didn't have enough fun.'"

I contradicted her. "'She knuckled down.'"

I did not know what would become of me. My classmates were now earnest graduates of law or medical school, while I dawdled in Central Europe, imagining myself into the purposeful lives of the women my grandmother loved to read. Within a decade of their journeys after the war, they would be eminent writers, known by English readers throughout the world for their pioneering entry into the public realm, their underlined novels, pamphlets, and speeches still in Nana's library.

The peers they invoke in their journals were so famous that the diarists could not envision a day when the names would require an identifying footnote. And yet these women—Storm Jameson, Phyllis Bentley, Winifred Holtby, as well as the friends they cite with presumed familiarity— are almost entirely forgotten.

When Nell graduated from the University of Toronto, she was written up in *The Globe and Mail* as the only woman in her class to teach in Western Canada. I see her striding to work on the prairie, her hair wound around her head in sinuous plaits, her shirtdress billowing behind her. I hear her students calling out "Miss" respectfully as she writes the upper- and lowercase alphabet on the board.

How did she live alone in Saskatchewan? How did her family allow her to go off like that?

"How could we stop her?" was Nana's retort.

All that beauty and conviction: look what became of it. She, too, lies in the ground. So does one of the lovely daughters she bore, who starved herself and died before her mother. So does the professorial husband Nell wed impetuously after a three-day courtship in New York and tormented the length of their ill-starred marriage. She should have stayed home, the pundits in Toronto wagged their tongues. Plenty of suitors, but she was headstrong.

◆

This afternoon, as I got into the car on the way to the cemetery, I put up my hair. Now the back of my neck feels skinned by the bitter air. It is one year since Tam heard the news that became her fate, a year since she called me to say that the possible roads had narrowed to a footpath only she could take.

In New York, the winter day was unfairly brilliant and auspicious. The river, next to which I walked for hours, was studded with ice that fractured the light and flung it back to me. Over my head the occasional plane dipped and vanished into the sun. I longed to vanish, like Amelia Earhart, leaving no place to mark my end.

Instead, I marched into the nearest hairdresser and said to the woman who lifted my curls admiringly, "Cut it off." Then I watched with grim satisfaction as the pelts fell around my feet.

When I met Simon that night, he swallowed visibly to mask his shock.

"Don't say a word." I stalked past him into the bedroom.

But when even the last medical means had been exhausted, Tam's hair returned, while, hundreds of miles away, mine, too, began to grow back, with unseemly alacrity.

◆

There is my great-aunt's birth date on the stone. She and Nana, only one year apart. Did Nana ever feel as I do, axed like a surviving Siamese twin, the phantom half beyond reach but still present in some suspended, useless eternity?

People are starting to go, but I cannot turn away from my sister. As if departing from a king, I walk backward from the grave, a soldier in an honor guard whose watch is over but who will not relinquish her duties.

The wisecracking commentator within me fades. I am purely here, my heart a slippery fish, my bones splintering. The matter of which I'm made, the genetic material we share, is uttering its own refusal: I cannot leave her.

When the hum of the limousines grows louder, I turn around. My father, strangely protective, is helping my mother into the car. Hats, coats, and bodies around the grave have rearranged themselves like a kaleidoscope, pieces falling away from the center into rooms and lives that have nothing to do with Tam.

The first bite of snow stings my cheek. I want to rest, a dreamy sleep without this terror, the snow covering me tenderly, perfect crystals melting, then crusting into a patina over my temporal flesh, accruing in icy intricacy until I am a white testimony to my sister.

THREE

I HAVE ALWAYS BEEN INTRIGUED BY WHAT IS HIDDEN. As a child, I would stand behind my mother in the kitchen, forcing her to turn by crying out, "I want to understand everything."

Although I like to pretend I have sprung from the head of Zeus, unshackled by my family's idiosyncrasies, as soon as I come back I feel the press of my ancestors, demanding tribute for my neglect of their claims. My mind begins its speculations about how we came to be the way we are, un-chastened by my mother's refrain, "No one can understand everything. Not even you, my darling."

Nana's answer was more opaque. "Some stones are best left unturned."

I begged her to tell me which ones she meant, but I already knew the tenacity of her closed face.

On the steps outside my mother's house, I falter. An intuition, a warning pulse, stops me from crossing the threshold. I take a shuddering breath of conifer and cold. The door is ajar; I will myself to enter.

My parents sit apart in the middle of the living room. Between them, one low seat awaits me. My mother's chest and mine bear a pin of torn black ribbon, symbol of heartbreak. But Nana and my father have done it the old-fashioned way. The lapel of Nana's impeccably tailored jacket is ripped, expressing, I suspect, not only deference to tradition but fury. My father's white dress shirt is conspicuously gashed.

The air is redolent with perfume, tuna fish, and boiled coffee, while visitors swarm about us, talking to each other in the hushed, excited manner that premature death invites.

When he still lived with us, my father was pedantic about closing the curtains as night fell, although, since we saw no houses beyond the garden, presumably no one was watching. One of my mother's pleasures is to keep the curtains open through the night. I am distracted by the windows' twilight reflection—masses of people in the choreography of a party.

The long buffet near the kitchen holds ziggurats of food. A communal busybody with pleated cheeks asks me officiously if I would like her to make me a plate.

"Can't eat," I say, and look around to catch Tam's eye.

The sonorous voice I have been trying to quell makes its callous declaration: You will not speak to her again.

All those who approach loom over me. I greet their knees, subduing my panic, an inversion of the times my parents allowed us to mingle with the company for the cocktail hour.

My mother's oldest friend, Marly, steps even closer. "Sweetie, you look exactly the same. I can see you, toddling after Tam. Eve the rebel," she says to her husband in an indulgent non sequitur.

No wonder Nell went to New York and married in a weekend, I think mutinously.

"Tam never had an angry word for anyone," Marly continues, her face crumpling. "She was so good. And she loved you more than words can say."

Marly's hackneyed paean to my sister is superimposed on Tam's own words as our fight unfurls.

"You want it as much as I did," Tam said. "You just don't know how to work for it."

She was lying in the hospital bed, looking up at me.

"Tam," I protested. "I love my life."

"What life? Teaching obscure women about obscure women? You're in love with the past," she accused me. "What about Simon?"

"He's in the present," I countered.

"It's pathetic. You're jealous of me," she said suddenly.

I looked at my sister, her body emaciated and bloated, her destiny written on her skin.

Pity felt worse than rage. "I work hard, too," I ventured.

"I've always believed in you," Tam said. "But you're still teaching night school."

"Continuing education."

"You keep saying you'll move on, but you don't."

"Such a wonderful mother," Marly intones. "I loved watching her with Ella and little Gabe. Oh"—she cries out—"how will we manage?"

While I try to speak, Marly's voice does what I cannot do and breaches my mother's grief. At last she reaches out to me.

Immediately, I want to crawl into her arms as I did when I was little, wrap myself in her scent and amplitude. Until this moment, her arms have hung slack at her sides; she has worn the same dress for two days and no perfume for the first time in my memory.

One of Tam's gifts, inherited from our mother, was her embrace. For a methodical, conscientious sort, Tam had an exuberant hug, a homecoming in itself. I basked in that hug at airports and outside trains. Now my skin needs touch as an animal craving, instinctive, essential. But I cannot curl into my mother. Many people have come to see us, and I'm meant to welcome them with dry-eyed dignity.

"Eve," my mother proffers in a whisper. "You might do something with your hair."

I am stupefied.

"It's just—" She looks around for help; none is forthcoming. "You're allowed to," she explains. "Your father once told me that an unmarried woman can even wear makeup during shiva."

I can tell that I'm gaping at her.

"Don't look so wild," she says.

If Tam were here, she and I would be snorting vulgarly. "Can you believe Mummy?" she'd complain. "Trying to find you a husband on the day of my funeral."

A gnarled old man, renowned for his appearance at weddings and funerals to cadge a meal, materializes before me, mumbles the requisite solemnities, and heads for the food.

"Maybe he's the one," I say to my mother.

◈

My mother and I were standing side by side before the mirror in the lounge of the East Side restaurant she preferred, while Simon stayed at our table, choosing the wine. It would be their first meeting, and I was not optimistic. For my mother, the eros of reading was a personal affront, as if my riveted gaze were a pronouncement to the world that she was not sufficient. Syntax and meter, the furnishings of Simon's professional dominion, did not tempt her.

"To be honest," she began.

"He's spectacular?" I said. Nothing positive has been known to follow this introductory phrase.

"He's so—"

I fortified myself.

"—unattractive," said my mother.

What I was not able to parse for my mother is that a man's most seductive organ is his brain. When Simon starts to talk, I'm entranced. His speech is like a fingerprint: the unique pattern of him. From his mobile mouth, Simon releases effortlessly words like "withering" or "sibilant."

"Say anything to me," I'll goad him. "Say something banal."

He laughs, and that's another winning aspect of Simon.

His finding me funny is so much more valuable than beauty.

Simon is slight—make that scrawny—with black eyes and the pallor of someone who spends most of his life in a library or basement. He looks like Franz Kafka on a bad day. To quote him, "I'm a poster boy for the kind of Jew Hitler couldn't wait to exterminate."

Occasionally, I'll interrogate him about how much he must have suffered in his public school, where I know from British memoirs that rugby was the currency and being Jewish and intellectual a near-fatal combination.

But Simon loved school. He was such an obvious genius that everyone left him alone. As a result, he is a more subtle type of insufferable. Simon's view of himself is an accurate estimation of his strengths.

"Why don't you begin with the assumption that I'm right?" he once asked me.

"Why would you want to be with a woman who thinks you're always right?"

Which rendered him wordless, for once.

Simon's mind works in such an oblique way that I cannot anticipate him. Long ago, Tam and I distinguished between men who are interesting and men with interests: Is there anything worse than hearing someone drone on about opera or golf or the minutiae of his fixations?

Simon has infinite obsessions, but no need to share them. If I'm in an elevator with him, he might say, "That's the worst Schubert I've heard in a decade."

Then, of course, I have to know which Schubert he heard ten years ago. Being Simon, he can tell me.

Our banter is like a game of chicken neither of us is willing to call. Since he's in England for half the year, we do not see each other routinely. "Besides," I inform him, "I cannot live in a rainy climate."

"Noted," he says. "Writing her dissertation on British writers. Cannot live in Great Britain."

We are neither here nor there, immobilized on an Iceland of relationship, decisions adjourned.

No situation on this earth was more likely to drive my sister crazy. For Tam, indeterminacy was a moral failing.

In my mother's living room, the brief day is shuttered, sky waning to ambient light, when the arbitrary murmurs coalesce, a melody in a minor key. Someone thrusts a prayer book into my clenched hands.

I do not follow, but when my father and my mother stand, I stand. And then: it is our turn to recite the fearful words.

Naked, I mouth the syllables of the kaddish in a monotonous trance. I cannot believe we are now the ones speaking aloud into the silent, receptive community.

I'm too proud, I think, as the service ends and people take their leave.

"Eve, we want you to know how—"

"It's hard to believe that—"

"We've been thinking of you so—"

Inevitably, I flee.

Above everyone, the hall is an airy refuge. Portraits of Nana and Grandpa gaze at each other pacifically across the landing, as if to say: We made this family. We did our best. But such a matter is beyond our province.

I pass my mother's room, evade Tam's childhood door. Beside the laundry chute is the entrance to the third floor. My fingers are adept at disengaging the latch. I cannot remember when I was last in the attic, and yet I know exactly where to place my foot on the first steep stair. When I close the door behind me, I find myself in absolute blackness.

Slowly I ascend, placing each foot with care. At the top, a thread of moonlight outlines the wood ledge.

Turning the glass knob, I am in our old playroom, unadorned, toys scattered where Ella has left them. Here is the tiny dormer room where once—Tam and I were enthralled to discover—a maid had lived at the century's turn.

On this flowered window seat I would lie until dusk, reading the books that are still piled beneath the hinged lid: lives of nurses in the Crimean War, siblings who journey to faraway lands by sail, wand, or potion. Here, when I was dropping out of high school, failing every class but English, Tam held me while I cried and told me she was certain I would be like Margaret Mead, intrepid, singular.

"With a PhD as good as Nana's," she insisted.

"But not in chemistry."

We agreed it was unlikely.

My mother's decorating habit has not extended to the attic. On this braided rug, I lay under Laurie as he kissed me. If I turn quickly enough, I might catch a ghostly glimpse of him.

I breathe in an essence of dust and wood oil. In the crooked closet where Tam and I had our clubhouse are a couple of wire hangers. The attic's emptiness is not sorrowful but confers a perfect peace. Alone in the dark, I feel my body shed its carapace of grief.

Through the bathroom's doorway, the ancient, footed tub beckons. I used to stand before the circular stained-glass window, pretending to be a captain at the helm, steering the great old house to safety. Now I unfasten the hook, and the window swings open.

The winter air charges my skin. When I close the colored glass, I can hear the reassuring thrum of the heat. In the linen closet are the worn beach towels we took to the cottage every year. I feel the ridge of Tam's initial, and hers is the one I take as I slip off my skirt and pull my sweater over my head.

It is bliss to be by myself, bare. Mapping the length of the room, I notice the slap of my feet, iridescent in the low radiance of the filtered night sky. When I turn the clover-shaped taps, the water rushes out in a glistening coil. Rummaging around the back of the closet, I find it: Ballerina Bubbles, Tam's much-coveted Chanukah present of decades ago. I lift off the torso of the pirouetting girl and pour in all the powder that remains.

Mounds of froth erupt. I skim the surface with my toes and then step in, molding my back to the curving porcelain until the steaming water is scant inches from the top.

The silence, when I close the taps, is complete. I am going to stay here through the night, I decide. No harm can befall me.

In a second, I am twelve, stretched out on the dock of Nana's cottage, the sun glazing my back where I lie, dreaming of love, lulled by the lap of water against wood, a minnow flicking between the slats, the far-off drone of a motorboat signaling the particular indolence that only a dock in summer can impart.

I am trying to imagine kissing, picturing the tongues I have read about, hours of turning faces and someone's passionate hand. In my renewed innocence I am almost asleep when I sense rather than hear the opening door.

"Eve?"

I know Laurie's voice immediately but do not seem capable of speech. Instead, I sink further into the water's delicate embrace.

Laurie is too circumspect to turn on the light.

"You may sit," I say regally.

He perches on the hamper.

I can decipher his face and the two glimmers of his hands. Lacy shadows waver over him.

When I was in love with Laurie, I was maddened by the wait between his sentences. Now, hypnotized, I do not care. The quiet lengthens steadily; neither of us will intrude upon it.

I am savoring a rare placidity when Laurie says, "You cut your hair."

"It's growing back," I assure him, as if everything else will be as it was.

"Remember those nights we stayed up late?" Laurie says. "Eating the sugar cookies your mother kept in tins?"

I listen.

"You and Tam sat across from me, howling over something that set you off, an inside joke you never could explain."

Stillness.

"Is it warm in there?" says Laurie.

"I'm in the womb," I tell him dreamily.

But the bath is cooling. I would like to add hot water, feel heat stream beneath me in prickly currents, but I will not sit up. Suddenly, I am as self-conscious as my primal namesake, innocence dispelled, wondering how she got herself into this predicament.

"Do they miss me downstairs?" I ask.

He pauses, and the room's encompassing history reasserts itself: What is the present day? I have been here long before you, and I'll be here when you're gone.

"I've missed you," comes Laurie's reply.

I do not want him to break this spell by moving toward me.

But I have forgotten Laurie's grace. He raises the towel heaped on the floor and holds it like a screen in front of him. I walk toward the pale square until it is all that is between us; I cannot see his face. When I turn my back, Laurie's arms envelop me.

I feel his clad body behind mine, not with desire but with innate sympathy, two night creatures taking each other's measure. I want to stand like this, enfolded in him, Tam's towel damp against my skin, forever.

SECOND
DAY

FOUR

"Eve," Ben says urgently at the breakfast table, "I need to talk to you."

Startled, I scald my tongue on my tea.

Ben mimes that the subject is not for Ella's ears. As I look quizzical, my mother, her face gouged by heartache, walks into the kitchen and lifts the teapot.

"Mummy, let me," I say.

She is pouring tea into a used cup.

"Mum!" I rebuke her, moving the cup to the sink. I take a mug from the cupboard while Ben waits.

"Not that one," says my mother.

I have inadvertently set down a memento from one of Tam's press junkets. My sister's face is wrapped around the cheap pottery.

In my haste to remove the offender, I slam it against the countertop. A crack splits Tam's artificial smile.

"Eve," Ben says again.

He has aged well, I note, as if he were not merely four years older than I. His hair, a wavy salt-and-pepper, is becomingly long, and his wire-rim glasses lend him a rakish air. Ben is chair of the history department at Toronto's most prestigious private high school, and I'm sure that the girls who attend it dream of him at night. Chin in his cupped hand, he has that lost-puppy look Tam liked from the beginning.

Impulsively, I walk over to give him a hug.

Ben smiles. I have hoped he did not take sides in my final debacle with Tam. His devotion to her notwithstanding, it seems he hasn't.

"I need to speak to you," he says.

My mother is sipping her tea, captivated by Ella's chatter. "I'm not taking a nap today," says Ella. "No way."

"What is it?" I ask Ben in an undertone. "I don't like to leave my mother."

"I promised," he mouths to me.

I pad upstairs after him to the landing.

"I have something—" Ben says. He reaches into the inside pocket of his jacket.

My name is on the front of an envelope, the handwriting Tam's.

"—for you," he concludes. "Tam told me to give it to you on the first morning. 'Before anyone comes.'"

I can feel the heat in my face. Nothing seems more intimate than this envelope, my sister's name engraved on the back beneath my fingertips.

"Ella needs me," Ben says tactfully.

Ignoring the incessant opening and closing of the front door, the faint call of "Eve," I sit on the bed and wriggle my finger under the beveled edge of Tam's stationery.

On the card I withdraw are a few ornamental words, printed with a fountain pen as if they were a calligraphed invitation to a tête-à-tête.

For the half second between eyeing and decoding her note, my mind composes: "Eve, forgive me."

But what I see is this: "The last time we were together, he said, 'I want to breathe you into me.'"

I turn the card over pointlessly.

This missive is not a hasty scrawl to a sister in whom Tam had a sudden urge to confide. No, Tam inscribed these words as carefully as she did everything else. The strokes are lucid, symmetrical.

I force the card into its concealing envelope. Whoever uttered this sentence to my sister, it was not Ben, who, in giving me this letter, has lovingly fulfilled an edict that rocks my body as I press my knees to my chest.

"Honestly, Eve," says Nana's voice through my door. "You're expected. Now."

I drop the envelope into my backpack, zipping it closed. But my sister's words cannot be contained.

"I want to breathe you into me," my mind chants as I hurry downstairs. "Into me, into me."

◆

Tam and Ben were married downtown in an old synagogue revived by an alliance of preservationists and retired craftsmen, who had faithfully restored its wainscoting and stained-glass windows. The ceremony, the first to take place there in fifty years, was covered by the *Toronto Star* and the *Sun,* even meriting a restrained mention in the dowager *Globe and Mail.*

Tam wore Nana's wedding dress, fastened at the back with lace-covered buttons in a dense line from neck to hip. I did them up one at a time, struggling to fit the tiny ovals into their thread loops.

"How are you going to get this off when it's over?" I said in frustration.

"Ben will tear it off with his teeth," she told me airily.

We both laughed at the picture of Ben as ravisher.

"I'm not a reluctant bride," Tam said.

I thought it would be graceless to remind her that a mere six weeks ago she had cried in the kitchen after mailing the invitations.

"It seems so—" She'd hesitated then.

"Final?"

"Well, I should hope it's final," she snapped at me.

"Don't blame me," I said, "for your attack of nerves."

"I am not nervous."

"Are too," I told her.

"I've never been nervous in my life."

"Do you want to talk about it?" I said, in the voice of my mother's newest infatuation, a psychiatrist whose pomposity we would mimic, barely out of his presence.

"Imagine," Tam said, "if Mummy announced her engagement just after my wedding."

"She never will."

"Get engaged?" said Tam.

"She still likes Daddy too much."

"You're wrong. She's only begun to speak to him civilly."

"Sex," I explained. "Daddy is sexy."

"Eve!" Tam said, disgusted.

"He is," I persevered. "Unlike Dr. Sanders. Can you picture him in bed?"

"'And how does that make you feel?'" said Tam.

I was laughing. "I'd like to transfer him and his transference right out of this house," I said. "Then again, he's not long for this world."

"Meaning?"

"None of them lasts very long."

"True," she said. "I intend to stay married forever."

"Who said you wouldn't?"

"We're a statistic, children of divorce."

"Tam, what's bothering you?"

"Nothing."

"Ta-ma-ra."

She was flicking her nail. "Sometimes Ben seems old."

"He's one year older than you are. Anyway, wasn't your list 'mature, responsible, worships me'?"

"Yes," she said, "but—"

"Are you worried you'll be bored?"

"Not at all."

"Your great desire is your work. Besides, you can always take a lover."

Before I could tell her I was kidding, she said fiercely, "Ben is my lover," verifying my supposition. She stopped herself. "If you ever say a word about this to me—"

"I won't, I won't," I said in mock alarm.

"Or to my children."

"Your children! Are you—"

"Of course not," she said. "It's just—"

I waited.

"I'll never sleep with anyone else."

"Most people," I notified her, "have several boyfriends until they find the one they're looking for. You've already found him."

She looked marginally cheerier. "Do you think it's the same each time?"

"Definitely not," I said.

"This is such a tasteless conversation I can't believe I'm having it."

"Do the two of you—? Any problems?"

She flushed. "No. But I have thought of calling it off," she said suddenly.

All my life I longed for my sister to be more approachable. Now I found myself unnerved by her fallibility. "Did you talk to Mum about it?"

She looked defeated. "Mum admires me too much."

◆

My mother, mourning her daughter in the living room, has been deflated by sorrow, vitality replaced by a husk of resemblance. Uncle Gil attends to her with vigilance as she rests against him.

"Tam was extraordinary," says Mackenzie Stoughton.

I am on guard, scrutinizing Mac as if he were a stranger instead of Tam's producer for a decade.

Everyone from Tam's office seems to be in the house the day after the funeral. Even the cashier from the cafeteria is stammering to my parents in a mixture of English and Portuguese how sorry she is.

According to the sociology of this rite, I am deemed to be less broken than my parents. The television visitors say something awkward to my mother and father before pulling up chairs before me. They have come directly from the show and are still in their fevered postproduction state.

"Tomorrow morning," says Mac, "a full segment will be devoted to her."

I hope he is attributing my gimlet gaze to bereavement rather than the conjecture to which I am subjecting him: Could he be the one? Could the handkerchief he keeps moving to his nose as though apologizing for allergies signify a loss much more drastic than friendship?

Mac is introducing me to people, all men, whose names I recognize from the card accompanying an ornate fruit basket yesterday. To Nana's amusement, I had diagnosed acute

Anglo-Saxonism from the prevalence of signatories whose first names could also be last names.

When Nana broadcast her weekly "Science Made Simple," she was the only woman and Jew on national radio. Tam's work life does not seem very different, if these visitors are representative.

To check my parochiality, I put my hands together and touch them to my lips. Tam's colleagues experience my silence as if it were dead air, that most dire of television conditions. They interrupt one another to tell me their favorite stories of Tam, the time she disarmed a deranged writer who tried to choke her co-anchor, Harris, on a live show; her deft interrogation of the president who, to his chagrin, confessed his Lone Ranger fantasies to her on prime time.

My father and then my mother begin to listen, sustained even now by my sister's accomplishments.

"And that smile," Mac says.

Tam was not a conventional beauty, but she was immensely appealing, an everywoman raised one or two degrees above the norm. Magazines had boosted their newsstand sales by featuring her on their covers. She had a dazzling smile, one that transformed her face unforgettably. Tam knew the impact of that smile, which the senior litigation partner in my father's firm had declared, when Tam was still in high school, could charm a jury off its feet.

"What most impressed me," Harris says, in the same

commanding voice he uses on the air, "was her courage. She showed us all what real integrity looks like."

This canonical description of Tam aligns with my parents' version of their daughter. I am doubly expelled from the hallowing of Tam, first by our fight and then by her letter, a stone tossed into the cottage lake that shatters the mirrored water to the far shore.

I focus on Harris, but skeptically. I cannot imagine him in bed. His buffed nails and the fanatical crease of his trousers make him an unlikely candidate for mussed sheets. I, however, have never been attracted to the artifice of polished men. Maybe he's a tiger after he hangs up that bespoke suit.

Mac, lounging in his black jeans, is more my taste. But what was Tam's taste? And who could have dreamed I'd be framing such a question?

I look to Ben's reaction for cues, but he shakes Mac's outstretched hand in a perfunctory manner and is manifestly uninterested in Harris's reminiscing.

"Everyone grieves in his own way," my mother says primly.

Her platitude joins the others, puny words that cannot compete with those Tam left me, syllables I attempt to match to Mac's aging choirboy mouth or Harris's chiseled lips.

Eeny, meeny, miny, moe, my indefatigable mind

performs. Who is the one? Which of these men looks as if he were capable of saying to my sister, "I want to breathe you into me."

◆

Simon is the first man to understand the sway of language over me. The texture of words, the taste of them, savory sentences exchanged deliberately: well past the end of love, I can remember what each man said, lying rapt, translucent with desire, until the hidden words between us, the ones too intimate for daylight, revealed themselves.

"Why can't they realize the true way to your heart?" Tam used to say. "They think it's sex."

"It is sex." I defended my reputation.

"No, it's what they tell you in the dark," she said. "All a man has to do is lean across a restaurant table in low light and start talking."

Now, while Mac speaks to my mother and father, I am picturing Tam in the dark, a tableau constructed in three dimensions before my eyes. She is naked on a white bed, arched to meet the hands of a man whose face I cannot distinguish, her perky newscaster suit on the chair. The shades are drawn. She has called home to see that the children are settled. Now she and he can disregard the illuminated dial of the clock radio.

I see the back of his head making its languorous circuit and hear her voluptuous sigh as he crouches between her legs.

"Television is a tough world," Harris declaims, "but no one begrudged her success."

Tam's onscreen rapport with Harris was enough to make them the subject of gossip, to her annoyance. But it was Mac she trusted, Mac who supported her in the inevitable politics of such a rarefied occupation, whose wit engaged her enough to quote him.

"He's so Canadian," Tam said. "Upper Canada College, father a diplomat."

I strain to recollect whether her tone was one of amusement or ardor.

"Call for you," my uncle says. "Shall I bring you the phone?"

"I'll take it in the den."

Nana's glare incinerates me as I walk away.

◇

Across the street from the den is the house that once be-longed to a boy named Jay, with whom I had a brief romance. I would sit in his room, his windows facing Tam's, more fas-cinated by the oddity of seeing my house as if it were my neighbor's than by Jay himself.

"I don't understand what's so interesting about your own house," he'd grumble, trying to coax me onto his bed.

But the temptation of his stash of pot or his Day-Glo posters as a backdrop to coupling did not compare to the seduction of what was already mine.

I shook him off, unable to explain, even to myself, why I could stare for prolonged minutes at the facade across from me, waiting for my mother's or Tam's shadow to cross the upstairs landing—this view I had never anticipated that imbued daily life with an aching mystery. If I stayed still, I might see my father's car, a blue Rambler that had long ago joined the great junk heap in the sky.

I kept my vigil so staunchly that Jay grew bored. After-ward, in what Nana would have called a controlled experi-ment, I knelt at Tam's windowsill to look at Jay's house. But it remained merely a house, exercising no sorcery.

◇

"Are you all right?" Simon's English accent inquires from New York. He does not reproach me for my silence of the last two days. Simon and I argue genteelly about abstractions, but are puritanical in sidestepping claims of the heart.

"There's no good way to answer that question," I say, bewildered that the story he knows about my sister and me has been usurped by a surprise story, a pretender that supplants the tale of two loving sisters who had a terrible fight.

My quandary would appeal to Simon, whose academic expertise is postmodern theories of language. He takes for granted that the reader, opening a book, sets sail purposefully but can never conclusively reach land.

Through the lace curtains of the den, snow is falling daintily, a gloss on a pretty winter scene. The glazed windows lend the front garden an enclosed, precious look. As a child, I would race outside on a day like this to step into a fantasy counterworld, where I befriended fauns and eluded witches until salvation came. But across the pristine expanse of white lawn, a procession of this-world visitors continues to advance. And I am mired in a darker universe.

"You have a letter," Simon says.

"What do you mean?" I cross-examine him, as if he suddenly has the power to read my mind against my will.

"You asked me to check your mailbox," he says patiently, "and so I did. You have one piece of mail."

"Who from?" I say suspiciously—and ungrammatically.

He is interpreting my response and filing it under grief.

"Eve, we don't need to talk about it now. I'll save your mail for you. You can look at it when you get home."

"I am home," I say.

"Right," he answers briskly. "And I'm in New York, thinking of you."

Sometimes, in bed with Simon, I consider the two of us, expatriates in New York, and marvel at how brief the Canadian period of my life turned out to be.

Naturally, he disagrees. "You can take the kid out of the Empire"—he teased me once—"but you can't take the Empire—"

Given that the Empire's representative was at that moment deep inside me, I laughed, as he knew I would.

Simon is the university's youngest tenured professor of English literature. I, too, teach English, but it cannot be said that I share my field with Simon. He has deconstructed language and reconstructed it again, the substance of his mental forays so arcane that one needs to be a mathematician to appreciate it.

His theories have earned him the sort of prizes for which he is not even permitted to apply. I'm waiting for the pendulum to swing back, and Simon knows it.

"Someone should study us," I contend in our disputes on the topic, "the old-fashioned readers, sneaking our flashlights beneath the blanket of fashion to read as if the world depends upon it."

Unlike me, Simon revels in his statelessness. He is a citizen of literature, he claims. His parents came to England from Vienna, and he has no geographical dolors. "Attachments," he says, "are portable."

Simon is too urbane to acknowledge that he is stung by my inability to contemplate our life together with any degree of seriousness. I prefer to think of us ironically—an approach he should endorse. The fact that Simon has won, with relative ease, all he desires simply underlines my resolve to stay just out of reach.

Although we have known each other for over two years, the time I spend with him confirms our disposition from the start, a wariness on both our parts that is refreshing rather than a deterrent. I met him when he came to observe the class I teach on women's autobiography, a course for mature students. He was interviewing ordinary people about how they read. For a man whose writing is complex to the point of opacity, Simon is nicely accessible.

After he finished querying my students, he turned his attention to me.

The more discerning his questions, the more evasive I became. Why, he wanted to know, was I teaching American women the lives of British writers of the twenties and thirties? What did I find in Storm Jameson's autobiographies or Vera Brittain's testaments that was more persuasive than narratives of citizens of the United States? How, he persisted, did I expect stories of another culture to elucidate the lives of women who were looking for sanction and precedent within their own? And in what way did memoirs of English writers from between the wars speak to me as an American woman?

For a person who did not believe in geography, his exploration was rather confined.

"If you'd give me a minute," I said, "you might find out that I'm not American."

"I'm no Henry Higgins," said Simon. "Where are you from?"

◇

In my mother's living room, Ben sits with Ella on his lap. I find it hard to look at him. My own mutable love life has been defined by the bedrock of my sister's. Is it only now that her husband appears slightly out of place among Tam's glamorous set?

"Eve," Ben says. "Ella wants you. I can't get her to sleep," he adds. "Please."

Ben's benign manner has been appraised in print as the most excellent correspondence to Tam's drive. Their evident affection made their life together the subject of fawning articles about domestic bliss. The idealization of Tam's marriage was in the public domain for so long that I did not question it.

Mac and Harris shake hands ceremoniously with each member of the family. As they depart, Mac turns to me and says brusquely, "I'll be back on Sunday."

Then Laurie is sitting before me.

The room's sounds recede into a hum. I see his tapered fingers set evenly on his thighs and want everything back: my sister, our youth, desire uncomplicated by history. More than anything, I want the incomparable elixir of beginnings, the heady confidence that all yearning can be assuaged by one man's mouth and hands.

"Meet me tonight," I say to Laurie. My mind has reverted to the sly resourcefulness of adolescence. "Side door at six."

Laurie stands. "Your niece is waiting for you. I saw her at the foot of the stairs. Six," he says. "I'll be there."

◊

"Tell me a story," Ella demands. She is lying in her pajamas, eyes distant with impending sleep. "I'm wide awake."

The breadth of her forehead and her bowed upper lip are replicas of Tam's. For a moment I am woozy, tossed between my present self as I look at my sister's daughter and myself as a child, inspecting Tam.

"One you've heard or one you haven't?" I say, our formula.

"The milk carton."

"Again?"

Ella nods with satisfaction.

"One day," I tell her, "we were at Nana's cottage. I was three and your mummy was six."

"Like me," says Ella.

"Yes, this is a funny story," I say, as if in warning.

"I know the story," Ella reminds me.

"So what happens next?"

"Just keep going."

"It was lunchtime, and Nana had run out of milk. She

gave your mummy and me some change and told us to walk to Mrs. Edgar's."

"'And hurry home,'" Ella says.

"'And hurry home, or there will be no milk for lunch.' So your mummy and I walked down the road—"

"By yourselves," Ella chants.

"By ourselves, past Mrs. Lloyd's, past Stewart's Marina, until we got to the store. Mrs. Edgar gave us the milk and she said—"

"'Hold it carefully, and don't let it fall, or something will happen.'"

"Of course, we had to see what would happen, so as soon as we got outside, we rolled the bottle down the hill. When we got to the bottom and picked it up, it started dripping. We turned it right-side up, but it kept leaking. No matter which way we held that bottle, we left a trail of milk behind us."

"At first, you were nervous," Ella points out.

"At first, we were nervous. We were scared that Nana would yell at us. But the more the milk dripped, the funnier it seemed, until your mummy and I couldn't stop laughing. In fact—"

Ella, giggling, prompts me. "You laughed so hard—"

"We laughed so hard"—I am smiling with her—"that I peed in my pants."

Ella finds this hilarious and disgraceful in equal measure. "You were only three," she says.

She turns over, and I see that in her hand she is crushing a rag. I look closely. It is a shred of the paisley scarf I gave Tam, faded from repeated washing.

My chest constricts violently. I force myself to imitate Ella's breathing until hers deepens into sleep. And still I sit, watching my niece's small form rise and fall.

Against the incantation of the evening prayer, I am waiting in the den for Laurie's car to turn into my mother's driveway. The air is dark blue, the one color of winter as opulent with possibility as summer light. Silhouettes against the resonant sky, the far houses are black, while the snow has its own severe enchantment.

Laurie is taking me for a drive on a dare. I have challenged him to flaunt protocol, to carry me off, anywhere.

When I hear his car, I make my way to the rarely used side door. Laurie taps on the milk box until I open the inside bolt.

He grins.

"Bad boy," I say.

"Ready?"

He is driving a sporty successor to Lady, the silver convertible that picked me up each morning to go to university.

"This is not a grown-up car," I say in appreciation. I seat myself gamely, but the car provokes something more cavalier. Stepping out into the frigid twilight, I undo the buttons of my coat and fling it into the back.

Once, in weather like this, I was in an accident with Laurie. An approaching car rammed into us, and Lady's hood crumpled instantly, as if she were made of paper. We skidded in a dreamy circle until we lit on someone's lawn, inches from a formidable tree. While Laurie got out and began the necessary exchange with the other driver, I sat dazed in the front seat, watching this Canadian ritual— two men on the street, breath steaming, hands ungloved, fumbling for pens to copy down addresses and license plate numbers.

"Where to?" Laurie says now.

He has a plan. I can tell by the determination in his jaw, the ease of his hand on the wheel, already turning. The heat is blasting. The distinctive smell of Laurie's leather jacket condenses time. Cassettes are scattered at my feet, in the open glove compartment, beneath the armrest between us. For the next hour we will be inside our music, Laurie's other hand rapping the beat.

I do not pay attention to where we are going. The streets roll by, we slide around corners, then cross a two-lane bridge onto a narrow road.

Laurie pulls over. We are in front of my family's first house.

"Look," he says, pointing to the house across from us, "there's the Gregory house. And there"—he adds with brio—"is a Gregory."

Sure enough, a woman who could be the Gregory daughter my age steps through the doorway.

"How on earth did you remember?" I ask him.

He looks pleased.

"What other tricks do you have up your sleeve?" I say suggestively.

Laurie turns off the tape. "What would you like?"

It is so quiet. No cars pass us as we sit in the dark. I look at the house where Tam and I were born and cannot decide if it is comforting or calamitous to return.

We used to play with the Gregory children past dusk until our parents called us, name by name, forcing us to go inside while we pleaded, "Ten more minutes."

I can feel Laurie moving toward me. My limbs are stilled by cold, my heart quickening every time I rediscover his presence. I know he will not draw any closer without a sign, and I understand that, despite my braggadocio, I will not be able to kiss him in the car before the house of my childhood as if nothing has happened.

He studies me and turns on the ignition. "Home in no time," he promises.

I want to tell Tam I saw a live Gregory, and the window out of which our parents leaned so that she could take a picture of them on her first camera. I want to hug her living flesh, breathe the musky scent of the lotion she favored instead of perfume, her hair against my cheek.

And I want to anoint the altar of grief with a sacrifice, but I do not know what to offer.

FIVE

IN THE REALM OF SLEEP I HAVE ALWAYS BEEN CONFI-
dent of my capacities. Tonight, however, the image I have
suppressed is mocking me—Tam's small body, earth bearing down on her in consuming darkness. Frantic, I try to
assemble my sister, the geometric panels of her hair, the
rhythmic thud of her sneakers against the track, her calves
like pistons.

Or the way she bent over me in the early morning when
we were teenagers at the cottage. "Let's go swimming," she'd
say, as soon as I stirred.

"Tam, I just woke up. This second." I feigned a stretch. "We haven't even had breakfast."

"How about if you watch me from the dock?"

I reached for my book, lagging after her.

"Some lifeguard," she said, turning back. "If I were drowning, you wouldn't notice."

"I'd look up once in a while."

In fact, I loved to watch Tam's body knifing into the lake. Her compact strokes, as incisive as she was, made short shrift of the cold. She swam between our two docks as if someone were chasing her, disappearing briefly at the foot of the ladder to emerge at my side, dripping water over me.

"My book," I protested.

Tam smiled, humor reinstated by exercise. If she didn't jog and swim by breakfast, she was edgy for the rest of the day.

She wrapped a towel around her black tank suit and sat down beside me. The wood beneath us was beginning to warm. I lay back, ripe with inertia. "Is there anything like summer?" I said. "Name one thing."

Tam arranged her towel parallel to mine, reclining, eyes closed, her hands behind her head as I glanced surreptitiously at the just-discernible mounds on her chest.

How could such radiant health be defiled? Although I had disgusted her in the hospital when I asked to see her scar, I was trying to restrain my imagination, in which an inflamed seam meandered across the devastated landscape of her rib cage, restoring half my sister to profaned girlhood.

In my presence, Tam cried only once, brokenhearted over Ella's vulnerability to this marauder. We did not speak of the hazard to me, also kin, but after I left her bedside, I slept clutching my breasts so fiercely that I woke bruised.

Now I have a revised version of her body: Tam, turning over in bed with her lover. My immaculate sister on rumpled sheets, wrapped in a dissolving shroud, flesh falling from her bones in the teeming grave.

I, who am considered the sleep genius in the family, the one to glide at will into Morpheus's arms, glower at the second hand of the clock on the night table.

"You have a one-track mind," I say to the clock. It ticks on ruthlessly.

Even in her teens, Tam would crawl into my bed, trying to catch what we called my slumber angel. Without waking up, I moved over to make room for her.

In the morning she'd conduct her investigation, determined to master the aptitude. "Tell me how you do it."

"Yes, tell us," said my mother.

"One minute I'm here, and the next—"

"Teach me how." Tam dispensed with my blather. "I could conquer the world if only—"

"Tam," I said dryly, "you'll conquer the world anyway. Besides, there should be one thing I can do that you—"

"You know what Daddy says."

I whipped around to read my mother's face, but she seemed oblivious to the reference. My father liked to reel off the names of leaders in history whose ability to catnap enabled them to prevail against fortune's vicissitudes and the enemy's resources. Napoleon was his perennial favorite.

"Look where he ended up," I prodded Tam. "Your energy is daunting enough. They say insomnia and sexual repression are linked."

Tam's dismissive hand brought my amateur psychologizing to an immediate close.

◆

Jabbing the lamp switch, I sit up. I am ravenous, compelled to notice that my life is tethered to my body.

Tam used to wake me at midnight to escort her to the kitchen when she couldn't sleep. "That's the point of being a sister."

Sometimes she made a dessert soufflé, moving efficiently from pantry to stove, softening butter, melting bars of unsweetened chocolate, separating eggs. My job was to scour the mixing bowl with the edge of the spatula, licking it clean until the aroma of distilled chocolate emanated from the oven.

If I couldn't wait, she made shortbread, allowing me to pour in the entire package of chocolate chips and then eat the raw dough to her half-hearted protests. Both the addition of chocolate chips and the shortbread's unfinished state offended her law-abiding mind.

I get out of bed, shivering. After the artificial summer of New York apartments, I cannot adapt to the temperatures of Canadian houses.

"I'm a tropical girl," I would say to my father, begging him to turn up the thermostat.

"Eve," he replied, in the same tone each time. "You are not supposed to be walking around in a T-shirt in the middle of winter. Put on a sweater."

My mother set the dial at seventy-six the minute he moved out of the house. This week, however, she seems to have regressed. I find my robe in my closet and weave my arms into its tattered sleeves.

I want to wake my mother. I want her to guarantee, as she did when I was small, that everything will be all right. Bunching up the blankets, I would steal across the hall of our old house to my parents' room. One tap on the door and my mother would be there, custodian of my father's sleep. She'd scoop me up, finger on her lips, to return me to bed.

My mother smelled sweet in her drowsiness, of cold cream and hair spray, her own womanly fragrance. Pulling the sheet tight over me, she would smooth my hair in even strokes, singing of summer and water.

But tonight she is alone behind her bedroom door. The moon is gone, and the reliable city beyond my window gives no comfort.

◆

On the landing everything is dark. But when I slink down the stairs, the house is awake with me. I hear the grandfather clock in the living room, the furnace's low rumble, the electric urn's reheating water again and again through the night.

A cup of tea is what I need, not from the urn but prepared the way my mother taught us at the doll parties she invented. On winter afternoons, she warmed the miniature pot and cups, letting the tea steep for the obligatory minutes. Straining the gold liquid into the china with which she had played as a child, adding as much sugar as we wanted, my mother invited us into her fanciful world.

There was never a time when her kitchen was not a paradigm of abundance. My mouth waters in anticipation of the antique cookie tins whose lids can scarcely fit. Etched green glass jars were stuffed with figs or Medjool dates, their bursting skins pasted onto the inside glass as if they were trying to escape. Foil packets of every size were a freezer cornucopia.

In the middle drawer of the dining room buffet, my mother hid the treats she was saving. Every year, Great-Aunt Abby's handmade chocolate fudge disappeared, looted by Tam and me one day after its arrival.

Someone has left the light on in the kitchen.

"It's a desert," my uncle says when I push through the swinging door.

My pulse goes haywire. "You just scared the hell out of me."
Gil is sitting at the kitchen table in his pajamas.

"And you're in my seat," I say, elbowing him.

"It's bad enough that Tam is dead"—he moves over—"but there's not a thing worth eating in this house."

"You don't like mayonnaise with a little egg salad? You don't like pimento olives on frilly toothpicks?"

He holds up his palms, a supplicant.

"You've been looking for food in all the wrong places."

"You'll see," Gil threatens. "How much lox can the average mourner eat? Tam was such a terrific baker. You'd think that a master planner like your sister would have left us something."

"You're sick," I advise him, walking over to the pantry.

But the shelves are vacant. I open cupboard doors, slide glass panels, rotate lazy Susans. An expired can of baby corn, a box of dried-up raisins testify stoically to our diminution.

"In all the praise so far, no one has mentioned her cakes." My uncle looks at me intently. "Lighten up."

"Now there's a phrase I haven't heard lately. Maybe it's because I don't get to talk to you."

"Your mother is my first responsibility. What can we do?" he says. "Tam's gone. I loved her. We're stuck with it."

"That's all?"

"No, one more thing."

"Make it quick, because I'm starving," I tell him.

"I'm going to order a pizza."

"Gil, it's after midnight. I bet there's not a pizza place in the Toronto metropolis that delivers at this hour."

"In Canada, we call them pizza parlors. Bet there is." He takes out the phone book.

"Tell them not to ring the bell."

He dials a number, then another, and orders in triumph. "Such skepticism," he says. "What do you have to be pessimistic about?"

I roll my eyes. "If we had one of Nana's Neapolitan cakes—"

My grandmother bakes as if she were still snatching moments between experiments. Her cakes are slightly skewed, and the icing never makes it all the way down the side. On holidays, Nana made her Neapolitan cake. After it cooled, she would cut it into one-inch squares because otherwise, she insisted, it was too rich.

Gil and I could eat a cake between us.

"Whoever could have had so many pieces?" Nana would say when she came back into the dining room to find only scattered crumbs.

My uncle and I did not need to confess.

A faint knock announces the pizza. Gil returns, balancing the square box like a posh waiter. "Madame?"

We eat all of it.

"Finally, something healthy," Gil says, draining a glass of Coke. "Now talk."

"About what?" My mouth is full.

"How is Simon?"

"You cut to the chase," I say in admiration.

"I try to keep up, even across the continent."

"The answer is—"

He leans forward.

"—I don't know."

"Still don't know?"

"What am I supposed to know?" I am exasperated.

"I don't want to rush you," he says. "But there are these little beings called children?"

"You don't have any. Of your own." Five years ago, my uncle married Sybil, a widow with two daughters.

"I had extenuating circumstances."

"You couldn't settle down. And neither can I. Maybe you're my role model?" I say hopefully.

"Please. And I have more biological possibilities than you do."

"Show-off."

"Seriously," he says. "Aren't you thinking about it?"

"I'm thinking about it. But not very much." I pause. "Who am I being?"

Nana had a rule that children at her table were not allowed to say they disliked a food she served. When Gil was
seven, he famously declared of her shepherd's pie, "I like it.
But not very much."

"I'm dreaming of true love," I say to him.

"What's wrong with Simon? He seems like a good sort
of fellow."

"Just what I need. 'A good sort of fellow.' Is that what you
held out for? You dated every woman on the planet until you
found Sybil."

"Not every," says Gil. "What's really going on?"

My silence is weighty, and my uncle is no fool.

"Don't tell me," he says slowly.

"Then I won't."

"If there's one thing to learn from the situation we find
ourselves in now," Gil says, "it's that you can't go back."

"People do."

"You're not that kind of person. And don't forget, I was
still in Toronto when you went out with him."

Neither of us mentions his name.

"You left him for perfectly valid reasons," says my uncle.

"Refresh my memory."

"One: you wanted to get out of Toronto." A second finger
pops up. "Two: he wasn't smart enough for you."

"What? That's not a bit true."

"Three: he wasn't attractive to you."

"That's a total lie." I am flustered.

"Okay, that was the test answer. You fell for it. Has it occurred to you"—he collects our paper plates and napkins for the garbage—"that the shiva of your sister might not be the optimal time to begin a romance?"

"According to Mummy, I could meet my husband any day."

"Husband?" he says. "You're not thinking of marrying Laurie?"

"Don't take his name in vain. And since when have you lectured me about my personal life?"

"You're right, I take it back. I'm too old to be preaching to you. But you're my favorite youngest niece—"

I wince. Gil always called Tam his favorite eldest niece.

"As long as you know what you're doing," he says.

"I haven't a clue what I'm doing." I feel abandoned. "And I'm not beginning a romance—"

"That's what it looks like to an interested observer."

"—I'm continuing one."

"Ah," says my uncle. "As someone who changed your diapers when you were born—"

I want to be in bed with Laurie. I want to take him into my childhood room in my mother's house and lie naked with him until these days of dread are vanquished. My reason knows that nothing will bring back my sister, but my body is not interested. I audition words—"escape," "illusion"—but they are not credible.

"Excuse me for interrupting," my uncle says, "but you know what Sybil says. When one big thing changes, it's wise to keep everything else the same."

"Prudence. Not in my repertoire."

"I look at you," my uncle says, "and I remember holding you in my arms when you came home from the hospital. It's hard to believe."

"Gil, I'm five years away from forty."

"I don't know if I'm ready for that."

"Tam was making a real point of it. She looked so young, but it was going to get tougher. She joked about plastic surgery, about media women who came back from extended vacations looking extremely rested."

"I like older women," my uncle says.

"So does Simon. He finds old interesting."

"Beats the alternative," says Gil.

On the wall of Tam's office in a shiny frame was the firing-squad shot in which she always appeared—nine men in suits and my sister.

"Take me through it," I said, sitting on the couch to drink the coffee her assistant had placed before me.

"My version or Mac's?"

"Which one is funnier?"

"Mac's," she said. Tam stood up in her tweed suit and pointed. "Here goes: Asshole, asshole, good guy—that's Mac—cipher, me, Harris, cipher, asshole, asshole, asshole."

"Bad ratio," I noted. "Who's the king of the assholes?"

She didn't answer.

"More than one? How can you stand it?"

"There are also two ciphers. Don't feel sorry for me. They all love me," she said.

"How can so many assholes have the judgment to think you're fabulous?"

Tam sat down beside me. "They don't care if I'm fabulous. They love my ratings. When my numbers go down, so will their love, believe me."

"Scary."

"Not really. I knew what I was getting into. No one forced me to be famous, make a fortune, get up at four—" She smiled, rueful.

"What happens after?"

"Sooner or later, I'll be kicked off the show and have to do guest specials interviewing celebrities." Tam did not sound happy.

"But you've been here ten years. Don't they owe you some kind of tenure?"

"This is my world," said Tam, "not yours. If you're smart enough to have a good contract—and I do—they pay it out. That's the deal."

I could not adjust to the brutality of Tam's work life.

"Look at it on the bright side," she said. "I'll retire in my forties and be able to give my kids breakfast."

"I suppose. Although years of serving breakfast doesn't quite have the gravitas of Canada's premier anchorwoman."

My sister's sleek legs looked exposed next to my jeans. When she stood up, she was almost as tall as I am.

"I can't believe your heels. How many pairs of pantyhose do you go through a week?"

"About the same number you go through a year," she said.

"If that."

"You can afford to take the high road," said Tam, "because in your profession looking young is a liability."

"I wouldn't go that far."

"An aging woman professor looks as if she earned her stripes. But an aging TV anchor just looks over the hill."

"You can't believe that."

"I have to. They can get two young blondes for the price of this brunette."

"But all your experience—"

She shook her head decisively. "It's under the knife for me."

"What will you say to Ella when she sees that your face is a piece of raw meat?"

"Must you be so graphic?" said Tam. "For Ella's purposes, I'll be on a long business trip."

"What if I don't recognize you?"

Tam's fiddling with her coffee mug stopped. "If you don't recognize me, the surgery's a failure."

"You've already decided," I said.

"The only change is that I'll look like a better version of me. Hey, I've done my homework. I've looked at hundreds of before-and-after pictures. You're making this harder."

"Not fair."

"You are. I don't have a choice. Your problem," she said, "is that you've never had to choose between two things that matter to you. You just keep not choosing."

Tam's eyes were on the enormous clock behind me. "I have a meeting."

The window of candor was officially over.

◇

"Tell it to yourself," says Gil, yawning.

"What?"

"What Tam always told you. 'Age doesn't matter in your line of work.'"

I yawn after him. "Maybe it's time to go to bed. Again."

"I miss smoking."

"Me, too. What do you do when you want to be bad? You were bad for so many years."

"I did bad," he says. "I'm over it. When I'm with Sybil—"

I look at my uncle. I see him every year, and yet all of a sudden his hair is gray.

"You still don't think it will happen to you," he says.

"What?"

"Middle age."

"I feel the same age I've always been."

"Eve," he says objectively. "There will always be a man to fall in love with you."

"But?" I elongate the syllable.

"Love and work, Freud said. You've got to get cracking on the work."

"What is this—a conspiracy?"

"What are you talking about?" said my uncle. "And is there any chocolate in the house?"

"I mean that Tam's been on my case about work." I ignore the dilemma of tenses. "And no, there isn't."

"Maybe she wanted to see you settled. You know her definition of settled."

"My incomplete life plan was somewhat irritating to her," I say, an understatement.

"Not as irritating as it is to you, I'm sure."

"I fade in and out of caring," I say, trying to block the memory of an anxiety so paralyzing I was unable to open a book.

"You teach those women writers of the old country, right?"

"'The old country,'" I make fun of him. "I believe our ancestors came from Poland."

"It's Simon's old country," he says innocently. "Let's talk about Simon."

"Must we? What's so interesting to you about Simon anyway?"

"You're not obsessed with him," Gil says.

"That's the first problem."

"Maybe it's an advantage."

"I wish it were. I'm a romantic. And you know I always have been," I say in warning. "Now I really am going to bed."

"Good idea. How do you shut off this fancy light?"

"It's called a dimmer."

"I'd race you up the stairs," says Gil, "but I don't want to wake your mother."

"I'd schmeer you."

He folds up the paper and tucks it under his arm.

"If you wait a few hours, you can get today's news," I tell him.

"You know I can't go to bed without reading the paper."

Suddenly, I see him in his plaid pajamas, reading *The Globe and Mail* in the rocking chair at the cottage.

"Addicts of the printed word," I say. "If I had something good to read, I wouldn't have come down here tonight."

"One of the worst things about death," he says sotto voce, trying to tiptoe up the stairs, "is that at a time when you most need to read, nothing seems worth reading."

"Saul Bellow: 'We are always looking for the book it is necessary to read next,'" I whisper to Gil's back.

"Family hallmark," he replies.

"I can see it now. Mum is reading Colette. Dad's reading the footnotes to a new Churchill biography. Nana is rereading *Black Lamb and Grey Falcon*. And you're reading a chess manual."

"I am reading a chess manual," my uncle says. "And you?"

I am reading a note that says: "I want to breathe you into me."

THIRD DAY

SIX

I OWN NO OBJECTS OF VALUE. I WEAR VARIATIONS OF the same layers of black clothes and have lived in too many apartments to count them on both hands. But I still have notes passed to me in grade two, postcards signed by people whose names I no longer remember, doctors' reports with a personal postscript—anything that embodies my life in words.

I also have violet sticks of scented sealing wax, some with the wick unburnt, and seals with a carved rose or other pledges of eternity. I own the last sheet and envelope of crinkly paper, awash with pastel blossoms, that my father brought me from San Francisco when I was ten. In a red leather writing case is linen paper from my classical stage and pre-addressed cards to my parents, the postage outdated.

During the war, when Grandpa worked in New York, Nana wrote to him every day. The steady currency of my grandparents' devotion is stacked in a battered trunk under the cottage dining room window, the one through which we would jump onto the porch bed below.

I have love letters of a different sort, expressions of abject suffering or raunchy lust, and sometimes furious curtailment. I have one that suggests, "As you read this letter, put your fingers—"

I have one that says, "The rage I bear you is my precious treasure."

When I moved to New York, I would descend in the elevator to my apartment's mailbox, my heart as tremulous as if I were en route to a rendezvous. Seeing a gleam of white in the metal cutout, I meant to go upstairs like a lady, make some tea in one of the porcelain cups my mother periodically bestowed upon me, slit the envelope neatly, and sit down to read with decorum whatever words awaited me.

Instead, I ripped open the letter for my first reading, stood in my doorway, transfixed, for the second, and carried the letter in my bag to read on the train or in line at the supermarket until, by the end of the day, I could recite its strongest lines, whether they astonished or berated me.

A little arrow into the future, I would think, mailing my own letter in return, hearing the scrape of the mailbox chute as it grated shut—no more time to erase or recopy, to contrive the apt phrase that would keep or relinquish him.

During Laurie's high school trip to Europe, I was a beggar at the den window, pleading with the smug despot of impeded love for the mailman to appear. Only when I gave up did he manifest himself, a potentate in his authority to grant or withhold. However disciplined I tried to be, I could not wait until the letters fell, but opened the door, hand thrust out, speechless.

Then I cradled the mail against my body and walked to the kitchen, turning over the envelopes with an assumed nonchalance no one could see.

One morning, the thin blue airmail form materialized, sandwiched between my mother's electric bill and a circular, almost thrown away—I deliberately frightened myself—nearly lost.

I held Laurie's first letter to me as if it were incalculably rare. He was not a writer, but what he said was this:

"I have seen paintings in Florence and obelisks in Rome. My eyes are full of beauty. My heart longing for you, you, you, you, you"—emblazoned with such force that his pen had torn the paper.

◆

From my closet, Tam's letter taunts me, insinuating itself into my brain as a set of unanswerable questions: Why didn't she tell me when she could? What does she want me to know?

The charged sentence in my backpack is tormenting me for another, more shameful reason. I, who have never envied Tam, not for the medal naming her broadcaster of the year, not for her silky newborn children or her life with Ben in their big old house and garden, am jealous of my dead sister because she had a lover who could say to her, "I want to breathe you into me."

Simon does not believe in language that behaves in such a fashion. "The words of youthful love," I hear his analysis. "A dream of merging, a language illicit love must imitate to achieve the same density of desire."

"I love it when you talk dirty," I reply. I covet the kind of language he disdains, avowals that slice through moderation to the passionate heart. I am tired of Simon's nuanced approaches and retreats. I want to depose every piety.

I want to drive Nana crazy.

"Tell me a secret," I say to her, the second we are sequestered for lunch.

"You were such an inquisitive child," she replies, dipping her fork into eggs that are already gummy.

"Who was your first love?" I can feel my provocation barometer rising.

Nana tsk-tsks.

"Second?"

"I don't know what you expect to hear," she feints.

I picture her in a tennis dress, daringly cut to the knee. I see her bend to toss a horseshoe, the clang of metal against metal as she looks up, victorious.

"Tell me about Grandpa," I say.

"What about him?"

Were you happy? is my silent question. "How did you know he was the one?" I ask instead.

She says nothing.

"Did you know he was the one?" I amend.

Here is what I know: Grandpa called to congratulate Nana on her forthcoming nuptials the very day she ended her engagement. When he heard the marriage was no longer taking place, he said, "I'm coming right over."

As soon as he arrived, he made known his intentions. He was, according to Great-Aunt Abby, crazy about her.

Nana discouraged him firmly, telling him there was no hope.

To which he said, "If I want to keep beating my head against a brick wall, it's nobody's business but my own."

They were married the following summer. In all their years together, they did not raise their voices.

Today, however, my grandmother is dyspeptic. "We had different expectations."

This is a coded sentence, one of her store, signifying that in her generation young people knew how to be true to their promises, whether in marriage or employment.

Nevertheless, I persevere. "Nana, you won't evade me forever."

She affects not to understand.

"Pretend we are fellow scientists, studying the data empirically."

"In what field?"

"Love," I recommend. "Were you ever disillusioned with Grandpa? Fed up?"

"'Fed up'?" She scoffs at my slang. "I don't have much tolerance for speculation. Particularly now," she says captiously. "Given what might have been."

I do not know if she is speaking of Grandpa or Tam.

"If you mean"—she submits—"did I love him through-out our marriage, why, yes, I suppose I did." She sounds amazed, not by the confession but by its recital aloud.

And then she blushes.

Grandpa died when I was five. The chandelier's prisms cast miniature rainbows about the room while Nana allowed my mother to hug her.

After the funeral, Tam and I played tag around the legs of the milling adults. Panting in the kitchen, I stood by my-self, calling down the laundry chute, "Grampy, Grampy," when suddenly I heard his reply far below, in the recesses of the basement.

I told Nana insistently to come listen, but she declined, humoring me until I grew vociferous with frustration, cry-ing to my mother and uncle as they led me away, "But I can make Nana feel better."

"After his first heart attack, Dad asked the doctor," Gil said to my mother, standing together in the doorway of the bedroom to which they had consigned me for a nap.

"He did? How did he ask?"

"'Can I still be close to Mother?'"

I saw my grandfather in the hospital, a bulky contraption of tubes and levers covering his heart and preventing him from hugging my grandmother.

"Do you know what she told me?" my mother said in a low voice, as though offering a gift in exchange.

Gil made a responsive sound.

"Until his last day, she liked to sponge his back."

I imagined Grampy, shrunk to the size of an infant, bathed tenderly by my grandmother.

These delectable confidences ended when brother and sister went down the back stairs.

Now I scrutinize Nana as she holds her fork upside down in her left hand to press her eggs onto the tines in British fashion.

"But didn't you get bored?" I say.

She dismisses the question. "Bored? Eve, we had responsibilities. When we made a commitment, it was understood to be permanent."

Nana does not quite have the courage to add: Not like

you. "I hope you'll be able to learn from Tam's life," she concludes.

"I have no doubt she will," says my father, booming, as if entering stage right. "Come sit beside me," he orders, taking my hand to shepherd me to the living room. "No one's here."

"Where's Mummy?"

"Resting. She's very, very tired." His voice changes registers.

"Dad, how are you doing?" I notice that I ask in the same inflection I would use, shortly after the divorce, when my veneration of my father's public self was infused by the unease of watching him alone in his new house, trying to heat a snack in the oven, jovial in conversation as he fussed ineffectually.

"You and I haven't had a minute to talk. Really talk," he says.

"Really talk?" says Tam.

Like many fathers, ours is not notorious for his ability to translate unvarnished feelings into speech.

"Look, we have to be strong," he says. "We have no control over the input, only the output."

My past crankiness in listening to these words is replaced with gratitude that at least one element of my life is intact. Unlike my mother, my father appears reassuringly the same. Growing up, I thought he looked like a movie star, and I suspected, from the way my mother's friends inclined their heads as they listened to him, that I was not alone.

He paid no attention to such frivolity. When I asked him if he knew he was handsome, he seemed baffled. "I knew I could do whatever I set my mind to doing," he said.

It would have been considered deviant, in those industrious postwar years, for a lawyer to think about his face any longer than the time it took to shave in the morning and straighten his tie. Yet even in grief, my father has not lost his distinction, conferred by height and by a magnetism all the more compelling because he is oblivious to it. Both the charisma and his denial are responsible for his success as a confidant of bereaved families, whose trust can extend to three generations.

"How is life in New York?" he says. "Teaching going well?"

"Yes, Dad," I say obediently, regressing in an instant.

"Did you have any trouble getting the time off?"

"It wasn't negotiable. Actually," I revise, "they were nice about it. I've been there for three years, and they like me."

"I'm sure they do," he says in a voice so hearty I look around in discomfort.

"Where is everyone?" I say quickly.

"It's a lull," he announces. "Afternoon. People on their way home from work. You must be a superb teacher," he regains his thought. "You were always a great talker. Even when you were little. And a good listener, too," he says tolerantly.

I'm sorry that his pride depends on such flimsy support. Clearly, he has given up on his vision of a sterling academic career.

"We should talk," he says emphatically.

I signal my willingness.

"How are you doing?"

I shrug, as if I were still a truculent teenager.

"I know how much you counted on her."

The needle in my mind moves, in one second, from passivity to rage.

"She wasn't perfect," my father tells me.

It is such a kind thing to say that my eyes smart. I move my chair close to his.

"She was much too hard on herself," he elaborates.

I can only stare at him.

Which he does not notice. "Where's little Gabe? It cheers me up to see that kid. He's starting to look like her, don't you think?"

"Oh, Daddy," I say.

My father sobs, wrenching, hoarse gasps of unassuageable suffering.

I throw myself at him, wrapping my arms around his

heaving shoulders as if he were the child and I the inadequate representative of the real world.

His sounds are rusty. My eyes fill in helpless empathy as
the firmament cracks.

◇

Tam was the one who told me about the divorce. Neither of
my parents knew how to relay the news, a subject they discussed so frequently and in a tenor sufficiently heated that
Tam had successfully disentangled the story line.

"Act surprised," she instructed me, "but not so surprised
they'll think you're stupid."

"I knew all about it," I lied.

When they ushered me into the den and closed the door,
I was as ill with trepidation as the innocent I was pretending
to be. By the time they completed their stumbling narrative,
I no longer needed to dissemble. While they uttered their
sunny reassurances—"This has nothing to do with you and
Tam. We love you both, we just can't get along with each
other"—I managed to throw up all over my father's recently
acquired leather armchair, my mother's guilt offering to him.
Its buttery skin bore the faint parameters of my unsimulated

distress for a year, until my mother re-covered the chair and moved it to the basement.

Suddenly, people who do not know my mother or father well enough to have come to the funeral are crowding into the house, wanting to serve up original words that somehow congeal into bromides when they hit air.

Sitting on my mourner's chair, I feel as if I have been in this posture since primitive times, a statue before which petitioners lay the muck of fruitless language. The front door opens and closes continually, and a swill of syllables pours over me: other people's memories, their attempts to make sense of what cannot be explained.

"You remember Blanche," says my mother.

I muster a civil face for our old neighbor.

"Roy, nice of you," says my father. "Pull up a chair."

"For heaven's sake," Nana says. "It's Elizabeth Boyd. However did she—"

Just as I cannot say "thank you for coming" one more time, I hear the splatter of the mail above the din. Scuttling to the door, I am not surprised to find an envelope for me, unstamped. I tear the paper savagely.

On Laurie's card are pedestrian words whose impact is immediate.

"Call late tonight. I'll be home. L."

◆

Even as I explicate the lives of women who left their provincial homes to make their mark, I cannot deny the rapture of waiting.

"You're an addict," Tam would charge. She meant: To the incandescence of love, ambushed by every variant of longing.

Tam scorned my elevation of indolence to a virtue. She had a theory that women should marry young so that they could get on with the real assignment of life, which is work.

"Why do you think great men always had a woman at their side?" she said. "They knew: you can't get anywhere without a stable family life."

"What about Paris in the twenties?"

But Tam had only contempt for the life of bohemia, which she considered affected. "There are people who look cool and people who are cool," she said. "If you have time to hang around in a café, how much work can you be doing?"

I tried not to take her words personally. I was, and remain, a devotee of cafés. My passion for them is also a testimony to that perpetual lassitude that so unsettled my sister.

"How many books did Winifred Holtby write?" she grilled me over the coffee I demanded we order at a lowbrow diner near her production studio.

"Fourteen. Didn't you ask me this last time?"

"And how old was she when she died?"

"Thirty-seven. But she had no sex life," I said in my defense. "I would have finished my doctorate long ago if it weren't for sex."

The truth is: falling in love, staying in love, assessing whether you're still in love, and falling out of love can be a full-time job. Winifred had one unsatisfactory and very intermittent relationship with a man she'd known since her youth, who was damaged by the Great War and could not stay steadfast—or even in England.

Her most important love, by far, was her matchless friendship with Vera Brittain. And its great accomplishment, after sustaining them both through the irreparable losses of the war, was the way it released them to pour forth their work.

"You seem to know everything about her," Tam continued. "Why can't you wrap it up?"

"Because I can't."

"If I knew half as much," Tam said, "I would have written my PhD, turned it into a book, and done the talk show circuit."

True.

"Is it that you don't think you know enough until you know every single thing?" Tam is so earnest she is scowling.

"I'm having an interpretive problem," I said. Perhaps if I could find the correct balance of love and work, I could arrive at a point of view on Holtby. "Anyway," I took the offensive, "what's the rush?"

"You're joking," she said, searching my face.

"I wish I were."

"But Simon's so productive."

"What does Simon have to do with me?"

"Isn't he an inspiration?" Tam persisted.

"If you weren't," I said forthrightly, "why would he be?"

"Maybe you chose him because he's like me."

I thought of Simon at his desk, fifteen books open around him, papers on every chair and all over the floor. "No," I said. Simon didn't care if I finished my dissertation. In his view, an external honor has only instrumental significance.

"But aren't you ambitious?" Tam pronounced the word as if it were in quotation marks.

"Very," I said, to ward her off.

"I don't get it. What do you want?"

"Romance. Maybe when my hormones fade, I'll start to sprint."

"I never know if you're serious," Tam said. "Then why not just marry Simon? Do you realize how old you are? Thirty-five and two months," she said promptly. "Aren't you afraid someone will beat you to your topic before you finish those coffees?"

"No one, and I mean no one, cares about these writers in America. It's mine to lose, as you would say in your profession. So save your career advice for all those newly minted college grads who beg you for internships."

"What about money?" said my jackhammer sister. "Rent, food, travel. All those books. You're not being kept, are you?"

I looked at her with incredulity. "Me? Can you imagine Simon forking over a wad of cash and saying, 'Sweetheart, go buy yourself something pink and frothy.' Tam, I have a tiny studio, no possessions, I use the library—and I do earn a living by teaching, remember?"

"What about kids?" she said, unable to restrain herself.

"You've done one too many stories on the ticking biological clock. I know it's your job to be the older sister, but you have to trust that I'll manage. I have so far."

"I'd never forgive myself if I kept my mouth shut and deprived you of a family."

"I didn't know you could give me one." I smiled to make sure she understood I was teasing.

But Tam was in pursuit of her prey. "Tell me about Simon's family. Are they like us?"

"His parents are in England. He's an only child who was sent away to school when he was seven. And he knows nothing about us, either."

I did not want to admit to Tam that between Simon's

British reticence and my disinclination to consider him a boyfriend, we spent our time in an arrested present tense. Fortunately, he was not here. If Simon had been sitting with us, Tam would have found out everything, unto the tenth generation.

"You're impossible," she capitulated.

◆

"Call late tonight. I'll be home. L."

It was a letter that precipitated the history of Nana's contrition regarding her sister. When Nell traveled to New York for a lighthearted summer weekend, and met the retiring professor to whom she inexplicably took a fancy, and wed him without consulting anyone, she knew within a year that her marriage was a catastrophe.

For the first time in her heedless life, she wrote to Nana to beseech her, with atypical deference, for her sanction: it might be best, she proposed, for her to leave her new husband, despite her early pregnancy. Could she move in with Nana and her family until she got back on her feet?

Nana, who never quit a task before it was completed with excellence, or tolerated within herself a rash thought or injudicious deed, composed several drafts of her response before she sent it.

"Be loyal to those duties willingly undertaken," she wrote.

Since that day, she carried as legitimately hers the responsibility for the ensuing suffering of Nell's daughters.

Years ago, on an aimless Sunday afternoon, looking at shoe boxes of correspondence moved from one apartment to the next, I resolved to sort the notable from the trivial, to refine my collection to the essence of meaningful exchange. No more letters confirming hotel reservations of vacations long past. No more overtures from conferences not in my field.

Reaching into a box, I drew a routine note from Tam, giving me her arrival time in New York. The letter was eight years old. I tore it into tiny fragments and valiantly pitched the no-longer-legible remains into the garbage.

A second later I was subject to such thrashing anxiety I had to shove the boxes back into the closet and slam the door. It was all I could do to stop myself from reconstructing that letter, lying so poignantly in the wastebasket, my sister obliterated scrap by scrap.

SEVEN

At three in the morning, I am sitting opposite Laurie in a club downtown and west, a neighborhood I do not know. We are mesmerized, downing one bottle of wine and then another, like besotted teenagers on a dock at night, daring each other to leap into the water.

My heart has not quieted since I walked out of the house, into the booth of this underground club not unlike the cafés of our youth, where the way we moved and dreamed was the constitution of a new era.

Part of me is mocking the pathos of my return. But irony

is extinguished by desire, which will not be tamped down by any paltry appeal to reason.

The club dims until Laurie is a wraith—shadowed hair, gleaming eye, mouth engraved. He is dark, but I am ablaze, as if I have guzzled light, the reincarnation of first love compounded by grief.

The last set begins. After a single chord, I recognize the song Laurie played for me in his room the night our friendship alchemized into love.

An anarchy of refusal electrifies my body, scalp to sole, defying all the chastening elders who relish denunciation, who issue their trivializing edicts about maturity and acceptance and compromise.

I do not have to listen to you.

"Don't do it," says Tam.

Or you.

The lead singer takes the mic. "It was homeward bound one night on the deep."

Laurie sets down his glass.

The singer's voice wails. "I dreamed a dream and thought it true—"

Laurie's fingers cross the dented metal of the table. Between my legs is a metronome of coveting.

Stand, it says.

I stand.

Move, it says.

And I move.

If there is a price for what I am about to do, I'll pay it willingly—anything to be restored to this perfection. I lean into the space between us. My hands are on his shoulders, my body porous, bones aligned. When Laurie splays his fingers against me, everything else is banished.

This is the velocity of lust. We press into each other, defenseless.

Shift over, the waiters are gathered at the bar, watching. The singer has begun to improvise, changing keys. The door opens to a rush of icy air, but we are greedy. Laurie chants my name into my hair as if I must be his salvation.

I tilt my head to look at him. His gaze is unfamiliar. The crescents of his lashes descend to shield his eyes, and then his tongue is in my mouth.

I have expected an encounter with the novel, a first kiss in all its springy delight. But we are not new. Laurie's body may seem as it was then, but our kiss is stoked by mortality. Votaries, pilgrims, we are exacting revenge against everything wrong with this flawed world.

Laurie and I move toward the door, spellbound.

"Home," he says.

"Eve," Tam yelled through the bathroom door. "Your time is up."

Sixteen years old, I was getting ready for my first official date with Laurie. When I finally opened the door, my sister waved her arms in disgust. "It reeks in here."

"Too much?" I held up the perfume bottle.

She relented. "It will fade by the time he comes," she said, opening the window.

Cool air began to dissolve the fog of the mirror as I toweled my hair.

"How can you stand there like that?" Tam was huffy.

"Like what?"

"You've got nothing on."

"Every morning we get ready in this bathroom. And every morning I've got nothing on. I'm your sister," I told her. "Ta-da."

"Very funny."

"What's your problem?"

"My problem?" she said. "I'm not the one with the problem."

"And I am?"

"Look"—she pointed to the flat green box open next to the sink—"you used up all my blush."

"I haven't touched your blush in months."

"Well, you should have bought me a new one when you were done with mine."

"I'll buy you a new one tomorrow," I said expansively,

stifling any evidence that my swooning love was gamier for the undernote of Tam's ill temper. She did not want Laurie, whom she treated as a lapdog. But she had to be the first to have a boyfriend; we both acknowledged her hegemony.

Tam was not satisfied. "You know I hate it when my things are ruined."

"Your blush isn't ruined. And you shouldn't have lent it to me if you didn't expect me to use it."

"I said you could use it. I didn't say you could use it up."

"Tam, this is ridiculous."

"So you say."

We were not, I understood, arguing about her blush.

Laurie lifts my hair and pushes it back to bare my face. I take his lip between my teeth and bite. He pulls away and then kisses me with such intensity I am momentarily afraid.

"Not yet," I say without breath. "I know what to do." Not his house, and certainly not mine. "If you pick me up at ten on Saturday night—"

"Too long to wait," he says.

I will pay obeisance to my mother and my father until

nightfall on Saturday. Then I'll sit in the car beside Laurie, away, beyond language, the collapse of present and past that will be curative.

Looking at him, I tell myself the truth. I am a person who wants to strip the skin from my life, pare away the facade, whatever the consequences.

On trips abroad I would stand, riveted, before tin market stalls where great sides of pig hung boldly while merchants fanned away flies from the raw, red flesh. Or stop on the street to stare at a clump of fur and offal.

I had to see what had been hidden—the guts, coiled, steaming. Tam learned to summon me to the site of a corpse while she stood at a distance, appalled. No matter how intently I looked, I could not reconcile the distorted form before me with a once-living animal. Seconds ago, it had been a sinuous cat, stretching on a grassy sliver of the road, and now: bones snapped, clotted blood, pelt ground into gravel, what had been clandestine revealed to every passerby.

No queasy thrill, however, compares to the terror of this week, the intimate unraveling of my sister.

Before my mother's house, somnolent near dawn, Laurie raises his hand through the open car window in salute. "Saturday night. Ten," he asserts, as if to convince himself.

I do not turn around. Tripping up the walk, coat undone, I ease the front door closed behind me with a truant's caution. I will be in the kitchen, cupping my mug of black tea to inhale the pungent steam as I surface into the day.

"I'm not going to ask you where you were." Nana rends the peace, blocking my path in the hall.

"Good," I say, assuming a veneer of casualness betrayed by my swollen mouth and matted hair.

Nana is invisible behind the plastic tubs of food she is carrying. A stripe of masking tape on each bears her indecipherable handwriting. "But I hope you know what you're doing."

The echo of Gil's earlier words is deflating.

"What are you doing?" I inch past her.

"We have to eat tonight, don't we?" She rests the food on the kitchen table as she follows me.

"Why? Why tonight?"

I sound moronic.

"It's Friday." Nana is impatient. "Friday morning. Six a.m."

She looks as self-possessed as if she were about to deliver a lecture. "We don't sit tonight," she says pointedly.

For a moment I picture our family standing as we eat. Then I remember: tonight is the Sabbath, when mourning is temporarily suspended.

"You'd better pull yourself together." Nana enlightens me, "You have a half hour until people come."

"I'm not showing up this morning."

She arches an eyebrow. "Eve—"

"Don't tell me you're surprised."

She does not contradict me.

"Nana, lie to me."

"Even if I tell you it's wrong?"

"Even if," I affirm. "You taught us it's important to be consistent."

"Now don't you sweet-talk me. It won't wash, you know."

I know.

"What will you do?" Nana braces herself.

"Sleep," I say. "I'm exhausted."

"Nobody told you to—"

"You're right," I deflect her. "And, yes, I'll take responsibility for the consequences."

"Then there's nothing to say."

When I hug her, she is so light I could pick her up.

Nana disengages slightly less immediately than I expect.

As the morning prayer floats toward me, I burrow under my quilt, saying the words my father inherited from his immigrant parents to beckon the angels who would protect us as we slept.

On my right hand, Mikha-El. On my left hand, Gavri-El. In front of me, Uri-El. And in back of me, Repha-El.

White wings filter the daylight. I am standing at the center of a loft in a dress that shocks, no stockings, and a preposterous hat, about to embark on a journey. My students are throwing me a confetti party, with seed cakes and baklava, bidding me a safe return. They pile wedding gifts into my arms.

The groom is blurred, but I know him. Laurie's arm is around me even before the opening syllables of the ceremony. My parents are vaguely present, although, in dream logic, Nana has walked me down the aisle.

Tam is ahead of me, under the canopy. She is wearing a bridesmaid's dress and a matching bow in her hair, looking exactly as she did, except that she is made of light.

"You see?" I say to Laurie, elated. "It wasn't true."

Radiant, I savor the perfume of the flowers over our heads, the silver goblet, the aura of achievement, when Tam in her luminosity mouths some words I cannot hear. Although she is not entirely flesh, I can still read her face. She is admonishing me, first in a temperate way, as if she does not want to curdle my pleasure over a minor matter, and then with increasing anger as I ignore her and motion to the assembled guests that we proceed.

My sister gestures wildly, but no one else can see her. Rather, smiles of satisfaction abound; my change in status has been met with unanimous approval. The hordes surrounding us clap with excitement.

"Kiss the groom," they are calling out. "We want to see you kiss the groom."

Tam's half-mouth exaggerates what she is saying, but the more I stare at her, the more she dissolves.

Slowly, spitefully, everyone turns gray. Laurie disappears. My dress is red at the hem, color seeping upward until I am the most vivid apparition in the room. Then liquid scarlet begins to slip down my back, viscous filaments, while my sister's voice enunciates words, precise, explicit, meaningless.

FOURTH
DAY

EIGHT

Too late. Too late.

When I wake up, it is past noon. The dream has invaded my brain like a shifty criminal. I dress furiously, as the melodrama of Tam's note casts a baffling shadow over my lost morning.

Downstairs, I take a detour to the kitchen, lured by the tang of my mother's soup. I dip my finger into the pot and screech.

"Tam! I mean, Eve!" My mother corrects her exclamation automatically. Not that my sister was the type to contaminate the soup.

I am clobbered by the recognition that I no longer know what type Tam was.

"Do you need a bandage?" says my mother.

She is cooking. She knows where the bandages are. My mother has returned, at least for Friday night dinner, a command performance even after the divorce. "Families that eat together"—she adapted the proverb to suit herself.

"We start at six," she reminds me. "Sharp. You don't want to incur Nana's wrath."

"Added wrath."

"We count on Nana to hold things together," my mother says. "And her wrath over our missteps is one reliable way."

"Our missteps?" I emphasize the pronoun.

"You're not the only one she thinks is out of line."

"Was it hard to be her daughter?" I want my mother to surrender.

"You mean, is it hard? It isn't Nana's fault she gave birth to a hedonist. Even as we were fighting, I felt sorry for her. I was not the right daughter for my mother."

Touché.

Nana's austerity is intrinsic to her character. She asks little and requires less of the material world, for which I do admire her. All her life, my grandmother has been made uneasy by her mother's native lushness. Nana's ancestors passed along a Canadian thriftiness that resists the unruly heart. From time to time, Nana will announce: She has no patience for shilly-shallying and dilly-dallying.

Before Confederation, my family was in Canada. Nana has always conducted herself as the last heir of the British Empire. She pronounces the "h" in "white" or "why" like the Anglophile teachers of my childhood and has the chief attribute of aristocracy: no awareness whatever of her patrician carriage and habit of thought.

We were never rich but earned a stature that felt like wealth. Nana's cousins inhabited Canada from Victoria to St. John's, where they held the offices of council member or alderman. Such attainments were, as Nana's bearing implied, only to be expected. Her work as a scientist was unique to the point of talk, and yet if I questioned her about her accomplishments, she claimed they had all merely happened to her, a matter of luck or timing.

It is a maxim in the study of women's lives that remarkable women will ascribe their success to providence, rather than concede their struggle, over many years, against adversity. However skillfully I introduce the subject of her ambition or gift, Nana remains infuriatingly vague. Great-Aunt Abby says that by the time Nana was three, everyone knew she was brilliant, "a flash." I love the slang, which evokes the sepia photograph of Nana, Abby, and Nell decked out in identical organza dresses, ringlets adorning their small, serious faces.

In an essential way, Nana cannot be known. Like any unrequited love, she is all the more intriguing for it.

◇

Outside, light gilds the gray city, rendering it briefly beautiful. The trees are studded with the green cocoons of burgeoning leaves. Melting snow surges toward the gutters. Above me, the sky is flawless.

Everything seems drenched in futurity, but I am cleft: Why is the season intimating rebirth? Soon I will be baring my arms to the elbow, to the shoulder, sliding into sandals, while Tam dwells in a winter without reprieve.

Yet even as I am afflicted by remorse—for how can it be that I, her younger sister, am walking on the Toronto street while her unceasing enterprise is stilled forever—I am galvanized by a new vitality, practically skipping beneath the great arches of the trees as I head to the main avenue.

The world is soaked in color. I pass the glasses store, the pharmacy, and the arcade with the post office and coffee shop. These stores have been the object of my disparagement for their ground-floor modesty, unchanging window displays, and laminate decor. Now I am pierced by tenderness at the sight of them. On this block, at my mother's urging, I got contact lenses, debated between two lipsticks and bought both, drank my first cup of coffee, pretending I was a veteran, and mailed a letter to Laurie, running to the post office instead of the corner box to give the envelope a half-day start across the Atlantic.

My recollected life, my crucible.

As I stride, I am making a list: Look into teaching a continuing-education course in British women's fiction. Find an apartment in Forest Hill Village; there are a couple of late-night cafés clustered there, walking distance to my mother's house, until Laurie and I—

"What will it be?" says the woman behind the counter.

I am the only customer. The shoppers of crowded Friday afternoons are already setting their tables for the Sabbath. Behind the glass are frosted chocolate doughnuts, gingerbread men with blue sugar buttons, iced cupcakes.

Simon does not know the glasses store. He did not buy licorice string and firecrackers in Duncan's Corner Shoppe. He has never stepped foot in Coleman's Bakery.

The woman taking my order, her hair in a net, is the same one who bagged my after-school treats in high school, the one who accommodated my dashes on the way to the airport for the blueberry buns I could get only in Canada. I recognize her, despite the years, but after more than a decade I am blessedly anonymous, one of thousands who have passed through her portals for the desserts of birthdays and holidays.

"Three of those." I point to the buns, plump with preserves.

She lifts each bun from the tray, counting under her breath with the Hungarian accent I remember, and wraps it carefully in its own waxed paper sheet, positioning one after another into the cardboard box she has expertly assembled.

"Hold it up," she demonstrates, taking my money.

The mundane nature of this transaction fills me with thanksgiving.

"I was very sorry to hear," she says.

Whiplashed, I scramble to leave, forgetting to thank her. As I crest the hill above our street, impaled by a stitch in my side, I see the redbrick library, sanctuary of my youth, haven of my Toronto-loathing childhood.

What I need this minute is library luck, books that call out from the shelves the instant I pass them, a novel just released, the second volume of an out-of-print British memoir. Even in New York, I keep my Toronto library card in my wallet.

God of reading, heed my prayer.

I cruise the shelves, trying to silence my raggedy breath, unsure where to start. Fiction is not in its place. Records, tapes, and videos have dislodged the biography section, now at the back. The oak table on which I used to take research notes is cluttered with headsets and monitors.

Canada's self-consciousness about its culture has led to the tagging of all homegrown volumes with a red maple leaf, a chauvinism unthinkable in America or England. I am scanning the top shelf and the lowest, applying my theory that the best books at eye level have already been borrowed.

Nothing.

Midway, under "M," is the journal of a woman pioneer of Upper Canada. Perhaps I should reread her account of life in the bush, a guide to lighting out into uncharted territory. But skimming the terse entries, I do not find wisdom. Once again, she clears rocks, feeds slop to pigs: not one leap from the quotidian.

I move like a crab along the aisle, but the spines are toneless, interchangeable, no snap of "choose me." At the bookend, straightening up before I turn, I glimpse a man seated before a video screen.

It is three o'clock, but there, unmistakable, is the poignant curve of my father's back, his resigned shoulders. Founding partner of Toronto's preeminent law firm, emblem of first-generation accomplishment, my father is hunched over the table in the middle of the afternoon, contracted to ordinary, like a senior citizen passing time before dinner and bed.

I squint to focus, trying to identify what he is watching. A documentary, black-and-white: I can just make out the wasted bodies, odiously exposed, in the arms of American soldiers.

Even from my vantage point I know these images, Allied footage of the liberation of the Jews. Frozen before the screen, my father is self-medicating in his own bizarre fashion.

I force myself not to interrupt him. He will watch or read anything about Jews, especially Jews in jeopardy. Unlike Nana, who is fully at home in the country of her birth and never admits the prejudice she confronted, my father grew up above the store. He still feels he is in Canada on sufferance.

My body is gutted; no one but Tam can find this situation properly hilarious. Immediately, I am suffused with self-pity, consigned to a lifetime of solitary rue because my sister had the effrontery to leave me, with only her stupid secret to keep me company.

Retreating into the biography stacks, I wonder if I should challenge my father's irregular solace, when, before my eyes, face out, is the quickie biography of my sister, published when she reappeared on the air after Ella was born, the jacket covered with gushy copy about the woman who has it all.

The room's natural light is failing. I know absolutely: even if I stay for hours, I will not find the right book.

"Hi, Daddy," I say brightly. My voice is tinny, counterfeit.

He spins around, animated. "Hi, sweetheart," the old lingo, as he hastily stops the tape.

Why is he not in his office, meeting with clients to plan their estates?

My father unfolds himself from the chair, insisting that he carry the bakery box. We do not mention Auschwitz. Escorting me, he walks on the curb side so that I will not get splashed by an aggressive car. He is protective, and I am peeved. What is he doing in my mother's neighborhood?

"Guess who's coming to dinner," says my sister.

This is the time, before we lit candles, when Tam and I would squabble over whose turn it was to set the table. As the last of the winter day ignited the western windows, we dashed downstairs to fold napkins and place the wine cups above the knives. In the kitchen, my mother would be ladling gravy over the browning chicken and placating my father about the fact that again, and indeed every week, she was late for the Sabbath. His religion bug, as she called it, was decidedly not catching.

We are a faux family tonight, my parents artificially united, flanked by Nana and my uncle. Great-Aunt Abby has rallied herself to come. But Ben cannot be here. Ella and

Gabriel, exhausted by mourning they are unable to name, are already asleep.

As my father sings to greet the Sabbath, the melody transports me to the cottage, my just-washed hair dampening the back of my shirt as Tam and I harmonize while the lake turns from silver to black.

"I want to breathe you into me," her letter states, insidiously.

I want her out of my brain.

Nana is at the table with her sister. Gil is at the table with his sister. But on the other side of my father, Tam's chair is empty.

Looking at my reduced family, I console myself: by tomorrow night I will be lying with Laurie, eluding all comparisons.

I kiss my great-aunt and open my mouth to speak, but my father is impatient. He pushes back his chair, drawing himself up. All of us stand. As he begins the blessing over the wine, his voice is like a damaged record, the needle jumping.

I concentrate on the potatoes, heaped in a china bowl, salted skin delectable under the flattering light of the chandelier. It is all I can do not to dump the entire bowl onto my plate when Nana finally passes it to me.

Before everyone has been served, I stuff half a potato into my mouth.

Nana looks at me askance. I want to tell her that the

potatoes are sublime, restorative, but I am not willing to risk escalation. Already I am in the kitchen later, eating these potatoes cold from the fridge, rosemary speckling my lips, calculating how many I can pilfer before anyone will notice.

My mother eats little. No one says Tam's name, as if without the audience of visitors we have reached an accord not to mention her. I am waiting for the spasm of tension between my parents, the customary dissonance on this seventh day of peace, but the cease-fire holds.

"So," says my great-aunt, "how's life treating you in New York?"

"The same." I am wary.

"How is—?"

"Simon? Fine," I preclude her.

My effort is unsuccessful.

"I'm surprised he didn't come," my mother says.

"I wouldn't let him. I told him it was out of the question."

"How long have you been seeing each other?" says Abby sweetly.

I ask each person what he or she would like to drink, my childhood job, and go into the kitchen. The door I've swung shut does not insulate me from my family's murmuring.

"Let me tell you right now," I sum up inauspiciously on my return. "I'm the same person I was a week ago. And I'm not going to marry Simon just because—"

"There's no fear of that, is there?" Nana says tartly. "You gallivant into town, free as a lark, of all times to—"

"I must be a wanton woman"—I do not let her finish—"as you suspected."

My mother closes her eyes. Gil looks as if, with the slightest encouragement, he would take cover beneath the table.

"Scaredy-cat," I mouth to him.

With relief, I listen to Nana's condemnation. Simon, Laurie, death, and loyalty get their representative share of her attention. If I continue to goad her about my purported dissoluteness, perhaps my parents will send me to my room. But there is no Tam to analyze the scene with me, joint commentator on another Stanley Cup of domestic drama.

Dessert takes place in awful silence. In penance, Nana offers me a second piece of cake, although I have not touched the first. My father moves forward in his chair, presiding over a meeting in camera with no negotiation he can execute, while my mother, eyes watery, looks at him in appeal, as if he can again be the exceedingly responsible man she married, believing he could make anything right.

At the end of the meal, Nana helps Abby into her fur coat, two old women under five feet. While Nana grapples with the hook and eye beneath Abby's chin, Abby looks at my mother and chants in the singsong voice of a child, "I'm taller than she is."

Perhaps life sears a sister's archetype into one's soul at the outset, and nothing she says or does for the rest of her days affects the inaugural image. Whenever Nana speaks of Nell, she sees not an aged woman alone but the glowing girl who drew men magically.

Years ago, after we had recounted the Seder's tale of exile and liberation, my grandmother said to me, "Your hair looks like I could turn you upside down and mop the floor with it."

I must have looked dismayed.

"It's sticking out all over," she explained, as if her footnote made the original comment acceptable.

When Nana hurts me, which is not infrequently, her barbs feel less personal than wounds inflicted by other people.

"Do you know what this haircut cost?" I said then, recovering to defend my single vanity.

Later I heard her report the statistic to Abby. Nana and her sister remember when a five-pound tin of salmon cost a nickel.

There is a moment in the Seder when I, the youngest, would leave the table to open the front door for the prophet Elijah, messenger of a redeemed world. Tomorrow night, I will part from this family to orchestrate, once and for all, my deliverance.

◆

In bed at last, I imagine I'll be dreamy with anticipation, that gauzy suspension of vigilance. But sleep is my new enemy. Desperate, I try an old tactic, one I used on pallets in strange cities. I slow my breathing until I am in Nana's cottage, reading a novel, one of her favorites, while the porch planks beneath the rocking chair creak companionably.

The summer I turned eleven, with Tam at camp, my mother invited me on a grand tour of Europe's capitals. In a cinematic fantasy of mother-daughter rapport, we would flit from Venice to Rome, Geneva to Paris.

While she described our suite in London, she gave my grandmother a look that did not escape my observation. My mother was conjuring a vision of frivolity to lift the heavy-heartedness that subjugated me whenever my parents' disputes assumed their new character—a terrifying indifference in the face of which their words of recrimination and despair would have been welcome.

Nana listened as I tried, ineptly, to decline in a way that

would not hurt my mother. I knew instinctively that my trailing after her while she deliberated the fate of her marriage would undo me. Notwithstanding what I saw every day, I wanted the fairy tale, an invented past of peace in the house.

"Why not send Eve to the cottage?" Nana said.

My mother looked horrified. "She'll be bored to death."

Nana drew inward.

"Eve?" my mother checked.

"I want to be with Nana," I said, as amazed as my mother that I, who already longed to travel, was rejecting such munificence to spend a summer alone with my grandmother.

"Settled," said Nana.

My mother could not help saying to me, "When I was your age I couldn't wait to get back to the city. Soon you'll be sending me letters about how you're jumping out of your skin."

Obdurate as she, I would not yield.

Nana and I stayed by ourselves, faithful to our routine. She liked the first hours of daylight. I slept until nearly noon. We waited the requisite hour after my breakfast and her lunch before we went swimming, Nana paddling steadily in her skirted suit, her tireless crawl estimable, I imitating her until I was short of breath, emerging before she did to lie on my sun-warmed towel next to hers.

On the porch, I consumed titillating bodice rippers from the town library. Nana completed the *New Statesman* acrostic in ink. Occasionally, she would glance benignly at the lurid paperbacks beside my chair. It was as if she had declared an amnesty. Never before or since has Nana been so merciful.

She might tell me about her childhood summers at the cottage, about the Trent-Severn Waterway and the Kawartha Lakes, how she worked at a nearby dairy during the flu of '18 to build up her constitution, or about the way farmers and merchants, timber barons and travelers bought passage from town to town.

The waterway continues down the Severn River to Lake Simcoe, churning waters tamed by massive dams, and on to Georgian Bay. Its journey spans the distance between the Jews that Nana's family alone represented, and the rest of Toronto's Jews with enough means to summer away from the hot city in places like Bell Ewart and Roches Point.

How Nana's parents and grandparents found their way to this town, and why they were content to spend a century of summers in a place they must have chosen because its social life was cordially but certainly closed to them: these are among the mysteries Nana chooses not to dispel.

Long past supper, when evening descended with the lenience of a northern summer, light departing like a reluctant guest, my grandmother made me chocolate pudding, quivering in the speckled blue bowls she and her sisters had scraped clean with the same tarnished spoons.

In her presence, the reproachful voices were hushed. There was no one to save. Nana's reticence was a kind of tact, and I flourished alongside her.

At night she turned on the radio to Starlight Serenade; we played gin to its swing tunes. My contribution to her education was rummy 500, a game she sometimes allowed herself to win, to my consternation.

Then we would go out, arm in arm, to look at the moon. Both of us liked the harvest moon, hanging low over the water, a burnt orange whose monthly flux was dependably changeable.

When Nana went upstairs, I lay under the maroon satin quilt on the living room couch to read. Then I darted into my bed on the porch, clasping the hot water bottle she had placed beneath the sheet, until I fell into sleep.

FIFTH
DAY

NINE

Delphinium, foxglove, larkspur, rose.

Each beguiling word releases, like a crystal stopper from an old perfume flask, the seduction of reading. On this bed I drowned in tales of love, courtships on winding paths and hidden terraces, bosoms bared in English gardens.

Lavender, cowslip, valerian, may.

Light saturates my wall and ceiling. I stretch deliciously, then amble down the stairs. My mother will make me coffee. We'll lounge about as day compounds into evening, shiva postponed for the Sabbath until my story can begin.

But the kitchen table is strewn with breakfast dishes,

orange juice pulp dulling the inside of a glass, blueberry preserves staining the china, a napkin askew.

On the counter is a note in her writing: "At kaddish with Gil."

It is Saturday morning. The stove clock says 11:11. I am the sister and daughter who is supposed to be standing beside my mother to say kaddish. But even if I rush into my clothes, I cannot be at services before they end.

Communal prayer was my father's domain. On Sabbath mornings, my mother stayed blissfully in bed.

"It's her time," my father would tell us as Tam and I closed the front door to accompany him.

This shape-shifting of my irreconcilable parents—my mother at prayer, my father who knows where?—abrades my serenity.

I pour myself a glass of wine from last night's bottle, climbing the stairs to resume my delinquency. If she wanted to wake me, she could have. But a miasma of fear has conquered whatever well-being I have mustered.

I need to kill time, to slam together the accordion hours between Laurie and me until tonight.

At the pulse of his name, I know exactly how to spend this morning. Up in my room, alone in the house, I will read every one of his love letters.

Nerviness subdued, I feel quite triumphant as I sip my

wine, which has improved overnight. Like me, I think to my-self. I will take down the hatbox in my closet, unfold each of the letters whose postmarks I once knew by heart, and review them line by line.

"You, you, you, you, you."

I have not sat on the tufted stool of my vanity for years, but my mother will not part with this furniture. It was hers when she was a little girl, and she claims to be saving it for my daughter.

Every time I come home, I backslide, pitching what I've worn onto the floor, my open suitcase buried beneath a mass of wrinkled black. I never hang up my clothes. And so it takes me a long minute to register what is amiss.

Resting my glass on the vanity, I am facing the rococo mirror, its enameled flowers and ropey metal vines framing a view of my closet's interior. But the highest shelf is bare. No hatbox.

I flip around to the closet to stand on my tiptoes, peer-ing, in case I'm wrong. But I do not see the outside curve of the box.

After the divorce, my mother gave up her annual appear-ance at my father's traditional synagogue and donated to the Salvation Army her collection of hats. I requisitioned a hat-box papered in blue scrolls and rosettes in which to store my letters from Laurie.

On my early trips home from New York, engrossed in the pursuit of love, I ignored the box. Why would I go to the kitchen and haul the step stool upstairs to exhume it? Every romantic knows that letters reread after the expiration of love lose their potency.

Now, in a rage whose acceleration is dizzying, I am obsessed with the idea that the letters are gone.

I stalk the house, opening closet doors. My mother's gypsy dresses, scarves, and jewelry are resplendent even at rest. On my father's side, I still expect to find his sober jackets hung on polished wings of hangers, shoes in martial pairs. But his closet has become a jumble of leftovers: an electric broom missing its dust cup, my mother's out-of-season clothes, fraying straw beach hats, an ironing board.

In the spare room, where my uncle is staying, the closet is vacant except for his shirts and a full-length photograph of Nana's grandparents. My uncle is as tidy and economical as he was in his youth. His leather kit bag, mottled and worn, is the one he took to the cottage or its exact replica.

Scampering past the uncurtained hall window, I tear down to the basement. Perhaps my mother decided to keep my few belongings in the cold storage room, where our camp trunks are stacked, net bags of potatoes and onions draped over them. I yelp as I stub my toe on the filing cabinet, containing all the household documents I would pore over sneakily: life insurance, my parents' will, our old report cards.

The hatbox would not fit into these drawers, but to honor the memory of my foraging I rifle through the files.

Even in summer, it's freezing down here. I shiver in my T-shirt and underwear.

In the third drawer is a crammed manila folder, its label obscured by homemade valentines and lace doily concoctions. I press the file's contents against the front and read the name on the tab: "Eve."

Here are my childhood clevernesses, saved by my mother. "When you girls are all grown up in houses of your own," she used to say, "I'll give you the beautiful cards and drawings you made me."

Although my apartments are temporary, I am nevertheless stung by the contrast in my mother's confidence. Tam's file is probably in her home office, not a paper out of place, while mine languishes like a spinster. I paw through misspelled Mother's Day cards and new year resolves to improve, but these relics only amplify my foreboding.

The edge of the metal drawer digs into my stomach. I have a third-person glimpse of myself, nearly naked in my mother's basement, and think I hear my family calling, "Eve, Eve."

Alarmed, I take the two flights of stairs so quickly I am

gasping on the landing. On the way to my warming wine, I pass the closed door of Tam's room.

It has been five days since the funeral, and I have not gone inside.

"If that hatbox is in your room," I say as I turn the knob, "I'll kill you."

◇

"Tell me how to be sexy," said Tam. In a week she would be seventeen.

I was reading on my bed, oblivious.

"Eve!" My sister looked down at me, demanding my attention.

When I am reading, there is a lag until sound turns into meaning.

"I want to know how to be sexy," said Tam, "and I want you to teach me."

I put down my book.

"How to be sexy," I repeated stupidly.

"It can't be what you wear," Tam said, "because you dress like a schlump."

Undeniable.

"And it can't be what you say, because you have an effect before you open your mouth."

"But when I open my mouth, it's better."

"Why?" Tam sat down.

"Because when they say something back, I can tell if they're interesting."

"I'm cute," said Tam, "but no one finds me sexy."

"How do you know?"

"I just do."

"Are you asking because you want a boyfriend or because you want guys to want you?"

"I don't see why that matters."

"Are you saying it's none of my business?" I said. "Because if you are, then don't ask me."

Tam glared at me. "It isn't any of your business, but if I have to tell you to get you to tell me, I will."

"Don't bother," I said, closing the book on my finger and getting ready to flounce out. "Because I have no idea what makes me sexy. Or anyone."

"Eve." She was imperious.

"You know, Tam, you want me to give everything away while you say nothing. But I'm finally too old to fall for it."

I was thirteen.

"I think you want a boyfriend," I said intrepidly. "And I'm sure you're going to have one any minute. Make up your steel-trap mind, and he won't be able to resist you."

"He is resisting me," she said.

Suddenly, I was mad at him instead of her. "Who is he? What idiot wouldn't see how great you are?"

"He likes me as a friend," she said. "What a cliché. But he wants to sleep with Marcie."

"Everyone wants to sleep with Marcie," I said. "But that's because she's willing to sleep with anyone who asks."

"Still," Tam said.

"Do you really want a guy who is the kind of person who wants to sleep with Marcie?"

Tam thought for a second. "Yes." Then she heard herself—and laughed.

"Is it Richard?" I hazarded.

She blushed so classically it was embarrassing.

"Richard," I confirm, "is the kind of guy everybody wants."

She looked at me with apprehension.

"Don't worry," I said. "I'm only at the flirting stage. But if you're not willing to sleep with him—"

"I'm not," she said.

"I don't know if there's any way you can get him."

"I need breasts. Bigger ones."

"Not even that would do it. And you'd look absurd." I was already a half foot taller than Tam.

"You're saying it's hopeless," she said.

I sat down again. "You have to act as if you don't care— and then mean it."

"I must have a boyfriend this year." Anticipating my question, she said, "Because I need to go hear TV journalists speak downtown when it's too far from the subway."

"You need a boyfriend so someone will drive you downtown?"

Tam nodded without shame.

"Taxis. Ever hear of them? Then you don't have to talk to the driver, or kiss him, or pretend to be interested in his brothers and sisters."

"But I'll look more grown-up with one," she said.

"Why is that important?"

"Because when I go up to ask a question, they'll take me more seriously."

"When you retire, will you live on the ocean side of Florida or the bay?"

"I have to be a broadcaster," said my sister.

"How the fuck do you know that?"

"No need to be crude," she said. "I want to be on TV by the time I'm twenty-five, and I'm already sixteen."

"So old."

"People who are very successful," Tam reported, "knew what they wanted to do at an early age."

"I'd better hurry."

"Ha, ha. Do you actually have any idea?"

"Ha, ha. Actually, I don't." I opened my book.

"Eve."

"Okay, I do."

"You do?" she said eagerly.

"I want to spend the rest of my life—"

Sloth was the biggest transgression in Tam's copybook.

"—reading in my pajamas," I said.

My hand on her doorknob, I am rescued by the phone.

"Hello," I say. A statement.

"Well, hello," says Simon. "You're out of breath."

"I am."

"Why would that be?" He does not sound like himself.

"What's wrong?"

"Why should anything be wrong?" he says. "More than what already is. How are you managing?"

Now I know what I hear in his voice: worry, an emotion not in Simon's inventory.

Before Tam bequeathed me her explosive little missive, I was proud of my faithfulness. Not for me the squalid secrecy of overlapping lovers and forbidden men. When I came home to Toronto, I could be a bad girl on high moral ground, leaving me immune to Tam's fretting jabs and Nana's censure.

"Look what's happened," I indict her. "You're turning me into you." A conniver, like a cheesy country song.

"I can't talk," I say to Simon, as if I have an urgent appointment.

"I'm noticing. Have you decided when you're coming back?"

My silence is telling.

"Because I'd like to meet you at the airport," he says recklessly.

You're breaking the rules, I want to cry, imagining him, roses in hand, waiting for me at the gate.

"If that's okay," he plunges on.

"Simon, I promised my mother—" Great. Now I'm a liar, too.

"Of course." He reclaims his dignity. "Will you call me when you can?"

"Yes," I say. Which is not perjury.

"Then I'll keep checking in."

So much for the man with whom I could never stop talking.

◆

Tam's room is not the lifeless shrine I feared. Ella and Gabriel have colonized it with board games and pull toys. When I open random drawers, I see that nothing is left of my sister. Unlike me, when she moved out, she threw away every childhood artifact. Tam was like a futuristic train, hurtling ahead in a whoosh of speeding silver. She loved a destination.

As a parting gesture, I fling open the closet door—where, on the corresponding shelf in her room, I find the hatbox.

Outraged, I clutch it as if Tam and I were in a tug-of-war.

"Mine," I yell like a lunatic. "Mine, mine, mine."

The letters, each in its envelope, look unimpeachable when I lift off the lid. Whatever they know, they are not disclosing.

I should have put a hair across the top, like detectives in the spy novels I devoured. The ribbons with which I had bundled the letters bisect each packet, but these meticulous bows are not mine.

I veer irrationally toward the idea that Tam is making me pay for my invasion of her secret drawer. "Pot calling the kettle black," Nana would say.

"I hate you," I say to her room, experimenting.

Until this week, I have considered myself a specialist in

complexity, but now I am demolished by the surge and recoil of fury toward my sister.

A gust of nausea forces me to the floor. I picture my outspread fingers tightening compulsively around her neck. I cannot know why she chose—as she was dying—to toy with me. But I do know this: any hard-won reciprocity between Tam and me has capsized. She is smiling smugly in the willful afterlife she's gained, and I am flailing.

The key turns in the front door. Gil and my mother are talking. I try not to slam Tam's door as I scoot across the hall, hatbox in my arms.

By the time my mother calls my name, I am safely in the bathtub, scrubbing my flesh with a loofah in penitential fervor.

TEN

AT LUNCH I AM FIZZY WITH DESIRE, A TWO-YEAR-OLD
with no attention span, food abandoned on my plate. I bat
away the image of Tam's gloating, cadaverous face. All I can
envision is tonight, when I open the door to Laurie.

"You were always bored on Saturday afternoon." In the
kitchen, my mother presses her lips together to blend her
lipstick. "Waiting for the sun to go down so Daddy would
let you go out."

My mother was the one who found the Sabbath unbear-
able, while I read on the couch, not noticing her or time's
passing.

"And you weren't bored?" I say. "You drove Daddy insane once you didn't want to keep it anymore."

"I'm not sure that was fair of me." She is thoughtful. "My family always did."

"So what happened?"

"I rebelled. And the more your father clung to it, the more I wanted out. I turned him into my police."

"But you must have talked about it before you got married. How you'd live. How you'd raise us."

"He took it for granted. And so did I. He probably reminded me of Nana. The enforcer."

"Given the sturm und drang," I say, "it seems the sort of thing you would have discussed ahead of time."

"But then I wouldn't have had you girls."

The incipient tears I see are not about me.

"Let's go shopping," I tell her. "Let's go bowling. Let's get out of here."

No, let me find Laurie this second, away from you. And you, I say to my sister. Especially you.

"I need a quiet day at home. Besides, your father's coming over."

"Again?"

My father must be the occasion for the lipstick. "Now you guys are in harmony?" I put my hands on her shoulders and swivel her around so that we are once more face-to-face. "How often do you talk to him?"

"Every once in a while."

"And he comes over?"

"If I invite him," she says virtuously.

Where is Tam when I need her? What would she make of this saccharine prospect? I feel the past widening behind me, a wake of retroactive possibility.

What am I mourning—my parents' marriage? My sister's conversion into a ghost vixen? Or the terms of our understanding, upended like ruptured tectonic plates, baring my feeble assumptions.

"If you could do it all again," I ask my mother, "would you leave him?"

I don't know if I want her to say yes or no.

"But we can't," she says, surprisingly gentle. "Do it all again."

◊

The last time Tam and I had coffee at Fran's, she had quizzed me as if I were a guest on her show.

"Tell me," she said, leaning forward engagingly. "Why are you obsessed with that period?" She meant the British years between the wars. "They would never have accepted you as a Jew."

"As if I didn't know. I've read their diaries. 'Oily Levantines.'"

"Would you rather live then?"

"A generation of women without men? Me?"

"But you're not getting married anyway," said Tam.

How could I explain to her, my seemingly logical sister, that the past has a bouquet, of white buttoned gloves, winter dusk, London streets, cloche hats, endless summer twilights in a Sussex garden, a walkway of pleached limes, and printed lists of privates killed in Ypres or the Somme. There are my women, as I think of them, striving to escape their Victorian upbringing, inventing their unconstrained lives, entering the public sphere with gusto, certain they had witnessed the war to end all wars—only to see within their lifetimes the ominous defeat of pleasure, virtuoso conversation extinct, a brilliant new world darkening.

Ages later, past eons of calculations, the remote stars finally pierce the sky. I have read every book in the house. I have paced. I have failed to nap. I have clocked the tempo of my parents' speech until this intolerable day of rest is over.

"Out," I tell my mother. "Don't stay up for me. You, too," I say to my father. They are about to take their seats in the living room for the final night of shiva.

"Elka wanted to see you," my mother says. "She's driving in from Brampton."

But I am gone.

Laurie's hand is assured on the steering wheel as behind us the city slips away. I remember everything. The lift of his jaw, the shape of his nails, his rolled-up cotton sleeve, the clench of his arm as we accelerate. To be lying with Laurie is all I want in this world.

As we fly through suburbs and then towns, the scale of the buildings diminishes until we pass only the occasional outline of a barn or shed. Soon there is nothing but forest and the dark absence of land that signifies water. I open the window. The loamy air of make-believe spring permeates the car as time unspools before us. Back I go as we move forward, Laurie's teenage mouth drawing nearer to kiss me, Laurie's face when I left him.

Snapping off my seat belt, I dare him to up the

speedometer. The car lurches forward, Laurie gripping the wheel.

I am thrust against him as if I were on the Scrambler, the amusement park ride that would tip us upside down above the world.

"Talk to me," I say, my hand over his thigh. "Tell me something."

"What do you want to know?"

I hear his quickening breath.

"What happened to your wife?" I ask him, inching my fingers closer to the V of his jeans.

"Not with me anymore."

"Where is she now?"

He does not answer.

"Go on," I say.

"You go on."

"What happened between you?" I expand my fingers.

"What happens between anyone?" he hedges.

"I'll make you tell me."

I lower my head into his lap and place my mouth precisely between his legs.

The car slows down.

"Steady," I say.

"She left."

◆

Laurie came to visit me in New York only once. For three days, we lay in my tiny room, never speaking of what was true: I was not going to come home, and he would not follow me. We made love incessantly, sated and desperate until daylight exposed the tousled sheets, the smudged glasses of wine, our bodies plummeting into stuporous sleep.

On the last afternoon, Laurie crouched at the edge of the bed and slid his tongue between my toes. I was mute with pleasure, interlaced by stinging regret for what I could not name, the signifiers he noted—cigarette butts, a fridge empty except for opaque bottles of beer, and no shade on my window.

Roused by my shaking body and the imminence of his departure, he cried, "You're in love with someone else."

But I was enchanted by my own limitless future, spilling into the humid summer streets of my chosen city, the gray avenue along which I watched his taxi recede toward the airport, to the original love whose clarity would not be replicated.

◆

"Beautiful beyond words." Laurie looks at me instead of the peel of highway.

Desire of this magnitude has an aspect of the terrible. What will happen after tonight? I think for the first time.

"You were in such a rush," he replied. "But who came back? And who was right?"

So this is our pact: we are going to pretend the night will have no consequences.

Laurie's face is smoothed by shadow, but his bare arm is lit and unlit as we drive. Beneath my clothes, my body is helplessly predicting its communion with his fingers.

We are almost there.

Under the night sky, our faces veiled by the mosquito netting on our camouflage hats, remnants of the Great War's desert conquests, Tam and I lay on the dock, telling secrets. Above our heads reigned Cassiopeia and Cepheus, who had so angered the gods they were consigned to spending part of each night upside down.

"In the olden days," I said to Tam, "our ancestors never knew if the moon would return."

The heavens were boundless, streaked by the Milky Way. Tam and I played the game we had devised. Nana was queen of the night; occasionally, we crowned her king. Our parents were the wavering constellations. On some nights, they were very clear, but then they disappeared. And we were Polaris, the North Star: constant amid the motion of the others.

Around us the water was glass. Small creatures nudged the twigs near the shore as the crickets, invisible in the scrub and stone, sounded their rasping meditations. On August nights like these, when the heat lingered into evening, my father would sit on the dock while the three of us swam naked in water that seemed tropical against our skin. It was paradise not to tense intuitively against the lake's early summer chill, the stars hovering.

My father, shoulders caped in his huge towel, lantern beside him and life buoy at the ready, was serious about his duties. Tam and I struck out alone with the thrill of the explorer until he grew perturbed and called us back.

"We're here, Daddy," we would call out, voices waterborne in a resonant duet, knowing, relieved.

He turned his back as we scaled the wooden rungs of the ladder to cowl ourselves in the towels waiting for us. Suddenly, we were freezing and had to run gingerly across the pebbled grass into the house to stand rigid under the near-scalding water until my mother knocked, laughing, to say we would use it all up before her turn.

I went to bed with wet hair and dreamed of magic, of gliding through the sky on the backs of lunar animals, of bodies becoming water, translucent with moonlight, our whispering on the dock an amulet against whatever misfortune might be in store for us.

With Laurie behind me, I turn the key. We move through the narrow hallway to the living room, shuttered for winter. Silently, we unhook the storms that face the lake as silver light pours in.

Laurie and I look at each other, not knowing how to start. Then I cast off my coat and begin to unbutton my shirt. Motionless, he watches as I tug at my sleeve and the shirt joins the coat on the floor. When I take off my jeans, I am not wearing anything.

Laurie eases his finger into my mouth and then touches each nipple with artful delicacy. But I do not want courtly love, elaborate with ritual possibility. No, I want to slam into him, body to body without imagination.

We have routed the ghosts of the dead to go back, blazing, delirious, soaked against each other as we stagger to my grandmother's bed to consummate this night in the only place we can, returned to our mutinous youth before anything sorrowful happened to us and the reproaches of adults were the amusing counterpoint to our bodies' ruthlessness.

"Mine," I say, jubilant.

Laurie kneels over me, sorting my hair strand by strand into an ornamental wheel around my head. He bends toward me, just as he used to, and then, effortlessly, as I close my eyes, he says, "I want to breathe you into me."

The ice cracking on the lake is the sound of Canada before humankind dwelled here. It was a great land swathed in ice a mile deep, ice that bestirred itself violently into our own age, heaving up spines of rock and water that fell from august heights into forced channels and riverbeds.

We of this century stand at the foot of an ancient pine forest on a bed of snow so soft, so entrancing we are planted for nine long months in the dappled midst of trunks too low to attain green. Then, for a brief wonder, we raise our heads, skulls lolling on our backs as if pleading for mercy, permitted to see the tips of the firs and cedars and, over them, a sky so passionately blue we are convinced: we can again survive this underworld so that, for scant moments every year, we may emerge into magnificent summer light, a light that transforms the towns and villages far from Toronto, grants them a condensed eternity as we make our way here, shed our winter skins to return to the children we were, the air whose purity revives our shrunken lungs—all the way back until death is merely the season's turning, inevitable, innocuous, almost affirming.

I know everything now, and I am not afraid. Laurie is kissing my mouth, a connoisseur. I am touching him as eagerly as if we were still each other's first, most tender love. When he and then I, an incalculable moment after him, begin, ecstatic, assuaged, our perfect descent, the name that I cry out is not his, not at all, but "Tam."

ELEVEN

I CANNOT REMEMBER EVER BEING THIS COLD. MY FIN-gers are so numb I need to fold them to button my shirt, dusty from its tenure on the floor. It, too, is icy, like a sheet hung on a winter clothesline.

I climb into my jeans, my back to Laurie, as modestly as if I did not know him and were forced to dress in the same room.

"When we get into the car," I say, "you are going to talk."

He is already clothed. "I don't understand how you knew. Did Tam tell you? But if she did"—he reflects—"you wouldn't have come here. What can I say?"

"Nothing in this house."

As I turn the lock, I picture Laurie and me as negatives, the reverse of the man and woman who opened the door, hallowed by conviction, light where there should have been darkness.

Laurie looks woebegone in the driver's seat. "Is it so bad? She was your sister."

"I'm the one with the questions."

He sighs. "If I tell you it was her idea, does that make it better or worse?"

It makes me think. And so, as Laurie pulls onto the highway, driving by rote, I enter the realm of unornamented truthfulness, in which I am alone.

No more dream of return, which has sustained Tam's life past its mortal end. Now Laurie is gone, despite the fact that he sits solidly beside me, and my sister is gone with a finality that does not resemble any insight I've had during these days of mourning.

Beyond the window, the disenchanted night, unbeckoning, inert, a corridor to dawn auguring nothing.

Why did you do it? I ask her. Why did you tell me and not tell me?

For Laurie, my silence is excruciating. "She wanted to know what it felt like to—" he begins.

My unquenchable curiosity has been temporarily blunted.

I relinquish him to you, I say to my sister. Anything to bring you back.

"I wanted to give her something that could never be repaid," Laurie says. "But tonight was not about her."

"Not true."

Ben's haggard face, Ella's gloved hand, Gabriel's sobbing: all this on one side of the scale, and Laurie on the other.

Why? I ask her again.

Tam does not reply, but her old words are as raw as when they were uttered.

"Everything you've done has been driven by what's between your legs," she said.

I was impressed by her unaccustomed vulgarity.

"How do you think I felt," she continued from her hospital bed, "hearing you year after year desecrate what meant the most to me, to Ben?"

Desecrate.

"Why do you suppose I didn't name you as Ella and Gabriel's guardian?" Tam went on, her voice in my head.

If I could reenter our fight, this time I would win; she had withheld crucial evidence.

"I meant every word I said," Laurie intrudes.

But I cannot remember any of his language.

"We met through her," he tries.

We met through her body. Her not-alive body, alive for

him as long as I lay naked with him, alive for me to make of the embers of a twenty-year-old love a conflagration fierce enough to repeal time.

"Talk to me," Laurie says. "We bumped into each other downtown. She had just heard the news and wanted to speak to someone she wouldn't hurt, not her husband or her parents."

Or me. I reappraise Tam's brisk delivery when she called me in New York to tell me there were no more choices.

"I hadn't seen her in years," he says. "She looked thinner, older, of course, but not ill, not"—he pauses—"dying. But she was."

I am the one who should be sitting across a café table from Tam.

"We were in a fast food place, where she wouldn't see anyone she knew. She asked me a lot of questions about my life, whether I was satisfied, whether there was anything I wished I'd done."

Did she ask about me?

Laurie perseveres, "It seemed only an instant since we were friends in high school. When I asked her what I could do, she didn't answer right away, as if she was thinking it over and wasn't sure. But I kept asking: Could I help?"

"And do you think you did?" I say coldly.

"I was able to give her what she most wanted. No one knew. We didn't hurt anyone."

My sister was the sovereign of standards, embracing marriage and work, disclaiming the lure of secrecy. But she took off her clothes for him—Laurie, the boy next door, the safe boy.

"I didn't know you had it in you," I tell him.

He flinches.

"Was it good?" I say.

"Eve!"

"Was it worth it?"

"She was going to die. She had been good all her life, she said, and she wanted to know what it felt like to be bad."

A light mist begins to film the windshield. Laurie turns on his brights. There is not another car on the road as we retrace the route by which we came, Laurie driving cautiously.

Now his hands on the wheel look peculiar, white undefined slabs.

"Eve," he tries again. "I want to keep seeing you. This may not be the best start—"

I can feel the laughter in my throat as demented hysteria.

"Take me home," I direct him.

"I made her happy," he says. "Can you begrudge her that?"

"I don't begrudge her anything." I am curt. "You don't know the story of Tam and me."

"She did feel guilty about you."

"This is making me sick." The complicity of their talking in bed about me. "My relationship with Tam is none of your business."

Everything is coming undone. I am not going to marry Laurie. I am not going to return to Toronto. My parents will have to fend for themselves. I am in the middle of the same life I had before, but I do not have a sister.

The tears that have made no appearance this week are blurring my sight. I don't feel immortal anymore. My knotted hair, the sweat congealed in the fissures of my body are the rank tracks of a story forsaken.

For a minute, I mourn the beauty of the idea that has borne me aloft, the lyricism of love, cleansed of dross or dailiness. Then, like a righteous suffragette of Nana's vintage, I see myself clad in a sensible navy blue dress, upholding the banner of merciless truth forever.

Simon will approve of my new position, if not the melodrama; he always favors the shredding of illusion.

I have not thought of him. Now I panic when my mind cannot recall his phone number.

I'm in Buffalo, I think, some limbo place between Toronto and New York, the future hazy and the past dismantled.

"I can't drop you off without telling you. You said you wanted to know," Laurie offers.

"But I do know."

I can see their story before me, frame by frame. "You went first to a hotel room, because she had never done it during the day in a hotel. You took the room yourself for the night, because she was much too famous. You left her the key and then walked out. She came half an hour later and went up alone. By the time you got in, she was under the covers. She didn't want you to see her without, with only one breast. But you told her she was"—I retrieve the language—"beautiful beyond words."

Laurie is looking at me, stunned.

"Keep driving. Her clothes are on the chair—no, in the closet. She was always neat. She's nervous, but you take it very slowly, asking her if she's all right. 'We can stop any time you like,' you tell her. But she says she doesn't want to stop. You are very careful. You're going to show her that it makes no difference, that—"

"No more," Laurie says. He has braked abruptly and is bent over the wheel, hands on his ears.

"I can go on," I say.

"No," he begs me.

"The next time was in your house. You had taken away any reminders of your wife. I see a scented candle. Again it is midmorning, after she finished her show. I wonder what you told your office."

"Lunch date. Back at two thirty," he says robotically.

"You wouldn't do it in your marital bed," I decide. "Is

there a guest room? Yes, but the bed folds out. The floor. The living room rug. How am I doing?" I ask him.

"Did she tell you? But she said—" He pivots. "You're a witch."

I am inflated by a momentary grandiosity. The clairvoyance lent by shock has resuscitated my confidence. I know my sister.

"She told me," I say.

"Are you sure?"

"How would I know otherwise?"

"But she said she didn't tell anyone. Not even you," he says, a perverse tribute.

"She didn't tell me in words," I concede.

"There's something else."

"What?" I am surly.

"It was a way of"—he gathers his courage—"of getting you back."

"I thought that was possible," I say. "But it turns out I was wrong."

"How can you be sure? You were always so sure."

"I sound sure. But inside I'm terrified. If I weren't, we wouldn't be here, trying to find something that was lost a long time ago."

"I never thought it was lost," Laurie says with vigor. "You decided suddenly, and then you left."

"Tam thought it was a mistake," I say. "My going to New York. She couldn't understand what I thought I'd find."

"And have you?" Laurie asks. "Found it?"

"What do you think?"

"You seem the same," he says. "Out of reach."

That must be the way he saw me then, the way I wanted to be seen. When I was a child, I tried to dodge my shadow on the midday sidewalk, to jump so quickly that I'd catch myself ahead of the foreshortened silhouette. I was always slipping out of my skin, a familiar eluding her magician.

"Winifred Holtby, come to my aid," I cry. But Winifred, golden, mythical even during her life, has been dead for over half a century. Her striking physical presence, her public voice, her passion for justice, her aristocratic renunciation of personal love, her unparalleled friendship: dust in a Yorkshire grave. She went home, all right, home for good at thirty-seven, her mother, her singular friend, Vera, and her political and literary admirers in attendance. Winifred was my age when, blind and failing, she could still tell her grieving mother that she and the permanently inconstant lover to whom she had been loyal since her teens had agreed to marry. And her heartbroken mother acquiesced in the delusion and congratulated her.

"You worshiped Tam," says Laurie.

"I certainly did not."

"You did. But I knew her in a different way."

"I'll say."

He hesitates. "I don't think it was that simple."

I prepare myself for a banality.

Laurie says, "I think she was jealous of you. Always," he says firmly.

My response is immediate. "That's not possible."

"Even sisters who love each other can miss the boat. Especially if they love each other."

Now—a little late, says Tam—I remember how Laurie's clichés went from endearing to infuriating.

I want to cry out: I left you because you couldn't speak English! But, of course, I sit voiceless.

We are nearing Toronto. It is still dark on this Sunday morning, but already I can hear church bells.

"She admired you for taking some chances, for not having a pat life."

This is not Laurie's language.

I tell Tam: Stop using Laurie as your ventriloquist.

"You don't know how much she berated me," I say, perplexed. "Even while the two of you were—"

"Sometimes it's that way."

"How do you know?" I am suspicious. "Did she use the word 'jealous'?"

"Maybe not, but I know she was. We both were."

I cannot accommodate Laurie's new loquacity or the content of his confessions. "No more talk," I say, slumping in my seat.

Laurie halts midword. I am remembering Tam's description of morphine. "I thought it was the euphoria of having a baby"—she giggled—"but it might have been the drugs. For an entire day, I didn't worry about a thing."

Once, I told Simon I was worn out from fighting for a little peace of mind. "I want to lie on a chaise on a South Sea Island," I said, "reading magazines and eating bonbons."

"That's what heroin feels like."

"And you know that how?"

"I was interested," he said. "Academically."

A half hour from my mother's house, I would give anything for the respite of an artificial oblivion. But I have to know the finale.

"Take me to Tam's house," I say, as we enter the last stretch of the highway.

"What will you do when you get there?"

What I want to do is to barge in, as the household is stirring, to declare, "Your wife was having an affair with my first boyfriend," compelling Ben to grieve not only for Tam but for his marriage.

I am appalled to realize how much I'd love to blow up everything, a frenzied anarchist. Inside my skull, a cacophony of malicious voices shrieks: It's your story. She didn't think of you; why should you think of her?

"Which way?" Laurie says. "Home or Tam's?"

"I suppose you know how to get to her house. Did she invite you in?"

He says quietly, "You know she didn't."

"I thought I knew a lot."

"This was not about her family. Or her husband."

"Then why?"

"It was about death," says Laurie. "Which way?"

"Tam's."

"Your force of life," he says, like a vitamin ad. "What Tam wanted to feel."

"A great marriage, a wonderful daughter and a new baby, fame and fortune weren't enough?"

"I guess not."

"Don't flatter yourself." I can't help smiling—and neither can he.

"Sometimes it is good to be needed," he says.

"Why didn't she turn to me?"

"In this one case," Laurie says, "you couldn't do what I could. Here we are." He stops. "Do you want me to stay?"

I run up Tam's driveway as if she were waiting for me.

SIXTH
DAY

TWELVE

"Wait up!"

Tam was a half block ahead of me, fracturing the dingy snow crust with her boot heel, unimpeded by her subsequent sinking into powder. She did not look back.

"Tam," I said. "Wait up. Can't we take a bus?"

Her face, turned to me, was adamant. "Step on it. Or we'll miss it."

We were walking, because we needed the exercise, Tam informed me, to the annual Winter Wonderland show at Casa Loma, the castle that was supposedly brought over stone by stone from Scotland to appease a homesick bride. Casa Loma was bedecked with fairy-tale Christmas lights. A boy soprano chorus of "Hark! The Herald Angels Sing" wafted above the parking lot as we approached.

I was panting.

Inside, a mob of tow-haired children in red or green velvet clothes was swelling within a cordoned-off area near Santa.

"The concert's upstairs," Tam said.

"Where's the cafeteria?" I needed hot chocolate, heaps of whipped cream freckled with cocoa. "My hands are ice."

"The show is at three," said my sister. "Cafeteria later. You're supposed to reward yourself at the end, not before you start."

I read in the *Globe* that if you offer young children half a cookie now or a whole cookie later, the ones who choose the whole cookie will be far more successful in life.

I knew which category I was in. And, alas, the one she was in.

"Is that the line?" I asked. "It's too long."

Children were snaking between braided silk cords as far as I could see.

"That's for Santa." Tam summoned a tone from her infinite reserve of disdain.

"I'm skipping the show," I said, lining up.

"No, you're not. Dad lets us come as long as we remember

it's not our holiday. Sitting on Santa at age ten does not qualify."

"I'll remember," I told her. "But I'm still going to sit on his lap. And ask."

"For what?" said Tam.

But I was not saying. It was a compensatory indulgence to aggravate her. A Barbie dollhouse even though I'm too old? A portable record player?

"And ho, ho, ho," I called after her.

On Tam's porch, waiting for daybreak, I would give all I have for an hour of her derision. So it must have been for Winifred—I see, in a glimmer of empathy—as she pined after Harry Pearson, her great love, despite her self-possession. If the pain of withholding is born early enough, it is so enmeshed with pleasure that the link cannot be severed.

A triangle of light, and Ben finds me, huddled before him, unable to stop shivering.

"I forgot that it's Sunday," he says. "No paper. What are you doing?"

"I—"

Ben looks winsome in his nautical pajamas. "You—?" he encourages me.

"I wanted to see you away from the house," I say lamely.

"How long have you been outside? Come in, come in."

The housekeeper, carrying Gabriel, is walking down the stairs.

"Please let me hold him," I say, dropping my coat so that the baby doesn't freeze. "You smell so good, Gaby," I murmur into his hair. "Where's Ella?"

"She's coming, too. Ella!" Ben calls up.

"By the way"—it occurs to me belatedly—"why aren't we sitting shiva here?"

"Tam asked me not to," Ben says. "She was afraid the kids would remember their home as a place of mourning."

As if her eternal absence would not suffice. But beneath Ben's sentence is the truer one I hear: Tam did not want Laurie to enter her house.

"Shiva is meant to be a consolation," I tell Ben.

"That's not the way she felt about it."

"And you always listened to her?" I cannot keep the sting from my voice.

"Always. I know there are aspects of Tam she kept to herself," he says. "But I didn't care."

"Why not?" Gabriel is fidgety in my arms. "Do you think he's hungry?"

Ben takes him from me and slings him expertly across his chest, patting Gabriel's back.

"How do you know that stuff?"

"You'll pick it up when you have to." His voice is tender.

"You were saying about Tam?" Despite my rage to deconsecrate Tam's memory, I am petrified that her betrayal will seep out of me, never to be retracted.

"We'll be late for services at your mum's," Ben says, "if we don't leave right now. I'll give you a lift. How did you get to our house?"

"A friend left me off."

"Pretty early for an act of friendship," he says. "Hi, sweetie. Here's Ella."

"Delicious." I open my arms.

In her car seat behind me, Ella prattles on, dominating the few minutes I have with her father. "What did you mean, 'aspects of Tam she kept to herself'?" I cannot stop, probing and poking about like a diviner.

"In every marriage—" Ben begins, and then remembers Ella. "Are you all right back there?"

I twist my head to smile at her.

"Mummy told me that when you were small, there was no such thing as seat belts, and it wasn't safe."

"But luckily," I say, "nothing happened."

"My seat belt is so tight it hurts my tummy."

"It doesn't have to be that tight," says Ben, eyes on the road.

"Does too," she insists.

"Do you feel safe and sound?" he asks her.

"How about ditching prayers?" I say to Ben.

"I'll tell you whatever I can." He looks puzzled.

Intuiting my zeal, Ella will not leave his side when we enter the house.

Come on, come on, I say silently. "Maybe you'd like to watch TV?"

"Just one show," Ben cautions. "Let's find one that suits you."

Ella succumbs.

In the kitchen, Ben and I face each other. "Now," he announces. "What is it?"

I am evasive. "There's only one day left, and you and I have not spoken about her."

"From the start, I was awestruck," he says.

"You and everyone."

"You think I don't know Tam's faults?" Ben pours himself orange juice. "Want some?"

"I guess you must, after all these years."

"I'm sure it wasn't easy being her sister. And sometimes it wasn't easy being her husband. Especially at the end."

My face prickles.

"The end of what?" my uncle says, pushing through the dining room door.

"The end of shiva," I recover. "Isn't it?"

"You can expect a lot of people today, so stick around."

"Where would I go?"

Gil looks at Ben, who is looking at me. "I'm out of here."

"This is a drawing room farce—but in the kitchen," I say to Ben.

"There is nothing you could tell me about Tam that I don't already know," he answers. "And there's nothing I want you to tell."

Abashed, I sit down heavily on the nearest chair.

"You're very smart, Eve. Yes, you are," he preempts me. "But the one thing you haven't tried in your adventurous existence—" He hears the implicit reproof and tempers his manner. "You haven't tried," he says more kindly, "the risk of living with someone through everything, including the problems that can't be fixed. Therein lies the unromantic nobility of love," he mocks himself with a flourish. "I knew Tam very, very well. You didn't have a monopoly in loving her."

"I never claimed to," I tell him. "You were her husband, for God's sake."

"Still, there's no one like a sister," he says. "Even a sister you can't talk to."

I start to cry.

"You don't know how many times Tam would be struck by something funny and have to call you when I didn't get the joke. I can see her laughing into the phone. And I hear you through the receiver, laughing back. That's what you need to remember, not how she let you down but how she turned to you. That's what I remember, too."

"It's not enough. Say more. We had such a ragged ending," I wail.

"We can't imagine ourselves in her place," Ben says. "No matter how dark your life may seem, you still expect infinity—all the chances in the world. To undo what you've done. To try something new. But Tam couldn't lie to herself or pretend. She was out of time."

On a bitter spring morning, Winifred Holtby was walking in the country, defeated by the knowledge, just acquired, that at thirty-three she had only brief years to live. Usually without self-pity, she was afflicted by the unfairness of her fate.

At that moment, she found herself standing at a trough of frozen water from which young lambs were trying in vain to drink. Taking up a stick, Winifred broke the ice for them. As she did, she heard a voice within her say, "Having nothing, yet possessing all things."

She strode down the hill with the exhilaration that, says Storm Jameson—another writer beloved of Nana—"springs from the sense of having lost everything."

I pray as ardently as a convert for Winifred's glory, the spiritual intoxication named by Jameson. Instead, Tam's words beset me, a galling inversion.

Tam had finished her first course of treatment, and we were bickering across a tiny table in an overpriced Bloor Street restaurant.

"Don't you think there's something ridiculous about living for sensuality into your forties and fifties?" Tam said.

I averted my gaze from her wig. "No."

"Why not? What about a husband and children? What about your dissertation? Lust above PhD: What would Winifred have to say about that?"

"Winifred had less sex in her life than I have in a month."

"Really? How could you stay interested in a woman with no sex life?"

I recorded her sardonic tone without comment. "That's one of many things that make her interesting. Like me and Nana. Can you think of any pair of people more opposite than the two of us?"

Tam acknowledged that she couldn't.

"Which is why she's fascinating," I say. "Why is Mummy so extravagant? Because of Nana's reserve. But I find her dispassion peaceful."

"Nana's tough," Tam said. "She invited Ella over last week, but by the afternoon Ella had read every kids' book and played every game. She told Nana she was bored. You know what Nana said to my daughter? Remember, Ella's five."

"What did she say? Can you find our waitress? My coffee's cold."

Tam ignored me. "'Ella, you're going to have to be more resourceful.' Then Nana unfolded the paper—and Ella was on her own."

"That's so Nana. What did Ella do?"

"She asked her what 'resourceful' meant."

"You've got to love the woman," I said. "Although she doesn't always love me."

"Nana is not exactly a live-in-the-moment person."

"Neither am I. I live in the past, as you like to point out. And I do have a plan."

"Yeah?" said Tam.

"I'm going to finish my book, keep teaching my women, and have a baby."

Tam jolted her cup. "With whom?"

"Whomever," I said glibly.

"Daddy would be proud of that 'whomever.' Remember how he made us look up words like 'inculcate'? Please don't tell me you'll be one of those single women who goes to a sperm bank."

"Why not?"

"Eve, men fall in love with you all the time."

"Not all the time. And I'm the one who has to choose."

"So choose," said Tam.

"Why do you care?"

"You're my sister," Tam said, as if that were an explanation. "Not some woman I'm chatting up about the latest lifestyle trend."

"Calm down. And thanks for implying I'm not chic."

"I am calm," she maintained, looking exercised.

"Will you be embarrassed to introduce me in Toronto? I can always leave the baby in New York."

"With whom?" she said, imitating my grammar and making me laugh.

"Truth? I'm not willing to give up on falling madly in love and having a baby with said person."

"Why would you think of having a baby with someone you weren't in love with?"

"Madly in love," I said. "One hundred percent gen-u-ine passion."

"Meaning what?"

"Meaning he has to be born within a year of me, so if an old song comes on the radio, he'll be able to sing it, too."

"But Simon is six years older, and he was born in a different country. So your very significant criterion disqualifies Simon."

"And that's why I'm not marrying Simon. You can expense the bill as firsthand research on aging single women."

"Yoo-hoo," says Ben, waving his hand before me. "Where are you?"

How can I tell him that the past is making guerrilla incursions into my life? Even if I expose her, my sister is untouchable.

"Anger is a poison; use it sparingly" is Simon's advice whenever I vent my annoyance to him over a dogged bureaucrat or petty tyrant.

As I refute him in my mind, the kitchen door bursts open again.

"You're not going to believe who showed up," Gil says. "I can't believe it myself."

Ben and I look at him expectantly.

"My glamour-puss cousin. This is worth the interruption. Live from Hollywood, Aunt Nell's daughter Sandra. Now going by the moniker of Alessandra, if you please. Feast your eyes." Gil points to the living room. "I haven't seen her since she was a child. She wants to meet everyone in the family. Your mother is mortified. So is mine. It seems Sandy doesn't quite get the etiquette of shiva. I suspect she has strayed from her roots. She's on her fourth marriage. Or fifth."

"How did she know to come?"

"She's filming in Toronto, and someone told her."

The living room is stuffed with people, but there is no missing Sandy. She has the aura of a woman who expects to be the sole focus of wherever she happens to be.

I scan the room to find Nana. Unsurprisingly, she looks shell-shocked.

Sandy's voice carries over the din. "I couldn't resist the opportunity to meet y'all. 'Finish the take and cut,' I said," quoting herself grandly.

I'm enthralled, in a sickening way.

"Darling," she calls out to me, "you must be Eve. Your grandmother was just telling me about you."

A likely story.

"Come, come, let me see your face. Yes," she says. People have stopped talking and are looking at her. "You have it."

She walks over to me and highlights my cheekbones with her fingers. "Did anyone ever tell you how much you look like—"

"Nana tells me constantly."

My grandmother would like to object, but she cannot deny it.

"She's my mother reincarnated," says Sandy.

In the living room light, I can see that Sandy is at least twenty years older than she first appeared, but neither the lines of aging nor the almost unnoticeable marks of the surgery she has undergone to offset it diminish her flamboyant allure.

"Come sit beside me," she says cozily. "There's so much to catch up on. I feel as if someone has given me such a marvelous present. Sit," she commands. "Let's tell secrets."

I sit compliantly.

"So who is he?" she says.

"I beg your pardon?"

"Who are you in love with?"

"Absolutely no one," I say.

"You have that look."

Now I remember that I haven't slept all night. What everyone else in the room is attributing to the travails of the sixth day of shiva, Sandy is, more accurately, registering as the aftermath of lovemaking.

"I bet you have men swarming all over you," she says.

"'Swarming' is an overstatement."

"But you're gorgeous," she cries. "The camera must love you."

"How long are you in Toronto?" I change topics.

"Two more days, and I'll be back in L.A."

"What role are you playing?" I ask Cousin Alessandra.

Tam, you don't know what you're missing.

"The older woman. The older, seductive woman," she says more hopefully. "So tell me about your sister. I hear she was a star."

"She was."

"Girl next door, ingenue type?"

"Exactly." I am beginning to understand that casting is Sandy's frame of reference.

"Tragic death too young?" she recaps, like a *TV Guide* description.

"You could say. Now tell me about your mother. She's a legendary figure to me."

"Mother was one of a kind. Uncontrollable. She had a dramatic life, you know. I guess you've heard about my sister," she says, and actually lowers her voice.

"Not very much."

"She was the family beauty. Far more than I," says Sandy, tossing her hair. "But unfortunately, she was brainy."

"Unfortunately?"

"If she'd been content to earn her living from her looks, she could really have gone places—modeling, acting, all doors were open. Instead, she had to try for a PhD. In anthropology, which no one took seriously. She was very insecure about her mind, and in the end it killed her."

I look disbelieving.

"Anorexia and pills. Very sad," she concludes, quite cheerily.

"Your mother was beautiful and clever. Wasn't she a role model?"

"Mother didn't do anything with her mind. Apart from teaching, which she gave up before we were born. Papa was the intellectual. She was always restless. Your grandmother was the brain in her generation. It was hard for Mother, coming after her."

Sandy's voice carries, but Nana is absorbed in pacifying my mother.

"Your grandmother had her youth," Sandy says. "But you know all about that."

I try not to show her how interesting I find this conversational arc. "Maybe a different version from yours."

She launches into the story. "She was crazy in love before your grandfather. It was a great romance—letters and flowers and trips to the country. Even a ring, a cluster of diamonds in a platinum setting. He made a big impression on Mother. Very elegant in his tennis whites."

"I'm confused about why it ended."

"Darling, he was loco," says Sandy. "Or so they thought. He would fall into these black slumps, and there was no reaching him. Maybe she could have put up with it, because otherwise he was the most charming thing, but there was another glitch."

I make a prompting noise.

"Inbreeding," she says, in an operatic whisper. "First cousins. Bad for the gene pool. They were very young. The parents broke it up."

"What happened to him?"

"Truthfully, I think Mother dated him for a while. On the sly. They must have been some pair."

"And then?"

"Never been heard from since. He was the type to die young," she says blithely. "But your grandmother must have told you everything."

I nod, in seeming affirmation.

"Promise you'll come see me in L.A. I'm longing to show you off. What do you do in New York?"

"I'm getting my PhD."

"Another one," says Sandy. "Is your whole family book-smart? Everyone reading all the time? No fun?"

"A lot of fun," I say protectively. "This particular occasion isn't fun."

She dismisses my sensitivity. "If you want a pick-me-up, just give me a call. Here's my card—" She extracts a turquoise square from her handbag. "Don't be shy."

Sandy stands up, inviting the room to watch her. She hugs my uncle one second longer than she should, kisses my disinclined mother and grandmother, and waltzes out.

"Well!" Gil says to me.

"Please don't tell me you fell for her. You'll tumble in my esteem."

"She is beautiful—" he says.

"In a blowsy way."

"Not my type. But what she had to say—"

"You were eavesdropping."

"Of course," he says, indignant. "Wouldn't you?"

"What do you think?" I dive in. "About Nana?"

"I'm remembering that she once spoke about cousins who lived with her while they went to university. Do I dare ask her?"

"I couldn't."

"I couldn't either," he allows. "But now when I look at her—"

"Hard to imagine her crazy in love, to quote Sandy."

"Not so hard."

We look at Nana and drop our eyes the instant she looks back.

"She's still scary," I say to Gil. "Admit it."

"She's my mother," he protests.

"So what?"

"So," he says, "I admit it."

"It's lucky Sandy didn't have that little chat with Nana," I say. "Nana would have made mincemeat out of her."

"Alessandra!" he scoffs.

"Snob," I offer in return. "She did solve one of the big family mysteries."

"Shiva can do that," Gil says sagely.

I am wary.

"You sit around together, and people tell stories. Stories you never knew."

"I'll say," I exclaim, in a tone so heartfelt Gil scrutinizes me.

"Any revelations you'd like to share?"

"Private recognitions, that's all." I seem to have become a professional dissembler this week.

"I hope they take you to a new place," Gil says sincerely.

"Now you sound like you're from the West Coast."

"Closure," says Gil. "Someone's come to see you."

Mac approaches my chair, looking ill at ease. Silent, he reaches into a small shopping bag to hand me a rectangular package.

I am under no illusions. It is the last full day of shiva, and my sneaky sister has one more gambit. For a second, I contemplate the idea of refusing to take it: in the postdeath competition, I want to win this round.

As if sensing my aversion, Mac drops the object into my lap. "Sorry I can't stay," he says, and exits like a process server.

THIRTEEN

"No more chances," said Tam, our last fight replaying, word for word. "Do you understand what I'm telling you? No more treading water, wasting time: all the stuff you do."

Tam's skin was blue across the thrusting bones of her arms. She strained to raise herself against the metal rails of the hospital bed. But when I moved to help her, she shook her head.

"There's nothing wrong with my life," I said.

"Nothing—except that you're squandering it. What do you have to show for yourself?"

"That's not fair."

"No husband," she began her catalogue. "No kids, and you're thirty-five years old. Practically no permanent address. A boyfriend you're no closer to than when you met."

I was trying to decide if her last point was true when she said, "You don't even teach serious students who are going for degrees."

"My students are serious," I said. "They just don't have our advantages."

Tam hears no irony.

"And I'm content with my lot. How many people can say that?"

"Truly content?"

"Tam, aren't you glad you've led your life in the way you believe is right? Isn't that enough?"

"You have a responsibility," she persisted. "To Mummy. And Daddy. What will they be proud of?"

"I'm not a drug dealer. Besides, you've given them enough accomplishments to last a lifetime."

We both refused the knowledge of how abbreviated that lifetime would be.

"How would it help to have two of you?" I said.

"What will they live for now?" was her rejoinder.

"You can't mean that. They'll never get over this"—I did not define "this"—"but they have Ella and Gabriel. And, yes, they have me, inadequate as it may seem."

"And what have you given them?"

"I don't have to give them anything. I can simply be. Their daughter, my students' teacher, Simon's lover, my own imperfect self. I'm still worthy. And your perfect self is all the more worthy."

"I'm not perfect," she said. "But it's so unfair." Her voice caught.

My self, smashed.

"Tam, if I could switch places with you—"

"It's no use."

I looked at her, questioning.

"You'll never change."

"Just because you're dying," I said, candid at last, "does not entitle you to insult me. I don't want to change, if I haven't made that clear. I happen to like myself the way I am."

"Because you'll do whatever it takes," Tam returned. "Emotionally. Going from person to person."

Adulteress, I think now, quaintly. Liar.

"You're hallucinating," I'd said suddenly. I was speculating frantically that the cancer had affected her brain—like Winifred Holtby's disease at the very end.

"I am not out of my mind. No, I've thought about it for a while."

"That I didn't care about the men I loved? Yes, loved," I said defiantly. "Is now the very best time to have this discussion?"

"There's no need to be sarcastic," she said, as if we were in high school.

"Let me get this straight." I sat down. "You're allowed to say what you want to me, and I'm not allowed to say anything back."

"No," said Tam. "I'm allowed to tell you the truth."

"Which is?"

"You don't know how to love."

"That's it!" I yelled. "You've gone too far."

Any minute, a man in a white jacket would come to take me away.

Tam's face was agonizingly unnatural, both swollen and excavated. "Why do you think I've never been able to consider you raising my children?" she said.

Your raising. "How about because they have a father?"

"Wrong," said my sister. "I was afraid they'd turn out like you."

"A woman who's cold-blooded?"

"Maybe not cold," she retreated slightly, "but not able to give wholly to one person. Face it," she said.

But I was not going to face it. I turned on my heel and left her.

I had imagined many last conversations with my sister, drenched in bathos, but not this one.

◆

In my room, I unwrap the brown paper as if I had ordered porn to my mother's address. I would love to hurl Mac's packet into the trash, but curiosity supersedes experience, as always.

Before me is a video, my name typed neatly on its label.

To watch or not to watch? The question is already rhetorical.

Under the bed is the accordion file that tails me on every journey: random chapters of my dissertation, the work perennially incomplete. I can recite by heart Vera Brittain's account of Winifred's final sickness, but I still do not know the end of her story—what meaning to ascribe to her life, to her death.

My room is a mess, the unmade bed tangled with clothes turned inside out, scraps of paper, and books opened every which way. As I toss blankets and sheets in the air, looking for the remote, I feel sick.

"Screw the remote," I tell myself, and shove the cassette into the VCR.

"Who's the real transgressor?" I assert to the empty room, building myself up for the viewing like a fighter spitting into his palms before donning his gloves to enter the ring.

The screen grows light. There she is, suddenly, alone in her hospital bed, looking at me.

"Dear Eve," she says, awkward and very ill. "I'm making this tape with Mac's help. I seem to need help for everything these days."

Tam is so small in the white room.

"By now you've figured out what I wasn't able to tell you in person. If you haven't, stop this tape and wait until you do."

Not very realistic.

"I don't expect you to do that. I couldn't." Her smile is quavery.

I need to lie down.

"If you're not furious, you're at least disappointed in me. I am in myself," she confesses, "except that I had to do it. I know I've been very judgmental about you when you've offered that excuse—"

I'll say.

"—but a person can be humbled, even at the end."

I peep at the screen through my fingers.

"Why haven't I called you? If you translate my pride into conscience, you may understand why I was so mean."

She sounds as if she's twelve.

"I can see you," she says, "already forgiving me. But don't forgive me so fast, because you'll hate me later."

This experience does not feel as satisfying as it should. Tam and I invented the cosmic callback, the vindication of a beseeching phone call from a lover or employer who had initially turned us down.

"I wish I could hug you," she says.

Tam is still in charge, because, of course, she can't hug me. I rub my sleeve against my wet face.

"I'm sorry I couldn't talk to you openly instead of arguing with you. I'm sorrier that I called you what I was afraid you would call me. I know you think of yourself as bohemian," she said, her voice fading, "but when I thought of confiding in you, I realized that you're the faithful one. I can't say more on a tape, which is only for your eyes. I would ask you to destroy it as soon as it's finished, but that's probably unfair— and I've been unfair enough."

She falls back against her pillows, breathless.

I'm so afraid she's going to stop speaking that I rewind the tape to watch it again. Automatically, I inspect her for subterranean clues to a deeper, different reality. But the second viewing rewards me no more than the first. This is my sister, as truthful as she can allow herself to be on the record.

I pause the tape to freeze Tam and put a pillow beneath my head, arms folded on my chest, legs aslant, copying her pose.

"What can I give you?" Tam says desperately. "What

haven't I told you that I should have?" She purposely modulates her tone. "There are two things I want to say. The first is: Simon's the one."

Simon. I try to imagine him as a living being, not a disembodied vapor from what used to be my present.

"I guess you're thinking I've lost my credibility."

Now that she mentions it.

"But marrying Ben was the smartest thing I did. I can see you sitting in your room, looking at the screen skeptically."

I am.

"I should be beside you, not on the screen," she says. "I bet you feel I'm trying to control you from beyond the grave. Well, I am. But just because I'm bossing you around doesn't mean I'm wrong."

More, I implore her.

"They'll be coming in to refill the morphine drip," Tam says. "I love morphine. Soon I'll need so much I won't be coherent. What can I give you?" she says again. "I wish I could visit you in your dreams. Remember we promised each other that whichever one of us died first would send the other a sign? But in case it doesn't work, or if you get tired of waiting, here's the last thing I want to say."

The last thing. Tam, stay. Say something trivial. Pick a fight.

"Ask Nana what happened in the decade between

Mummy's birth and Gil's. No, asking her won't work," she retracts her suggestion. "Sit with her and talk about losing what is irreplaceable."

The idea of having a heart-to-heart with my grandmother is even less probable than my breaking through the screen, in an old-fashioned movie, to enter into a real conversation with my sister. But I can see that Tam is losing her breath.

"I love you," she says. And the screen is black.

In soggy sleep, my face mashed into the pillow, I think I hear the phone ring. No one else picks up.

"You don't sound right," Simon says.

"What time is it?" I say blearily.

"You don't even sound like you."

"I need to be home."

"Home is portable," he says staunchly. Then he wavers. "Are you not feeling at home?"

"Don't ask me."

He asks me. "What happened?"

I flop back onto the bed. "All my certitude cells turned over at once."

"What are you no longer certain about?" he says, very gently. "What does a woman look like who has endured total cellular turnover?"

"Terrible. I'm going to the mirror to check."

A drawn, anxious-looking woman with stringy hair looks at me without sympathy.

"When are you coming back?" He has learned his lesson and avoids the word "home."

I don't know.

Simon does not seem to like my silence. "Isn't it over tomorrow?"

"After breakfast we take a walk around the block. And then it's over. But I can't desert my parents."

"Did they ask you to stay?"

I know they expect me to leave. Shall I tell Simon that I was thinking of getting an apartment around the corner from my mother and having dinner with my father twice a week?

The video's black edge is leering at me.

"Give me the day of your return. I want to be certain I'm in the city," Simon says. "Can I help you with your plane ticket? Do you want to use my travel agent?"

What is happening to Simon? If you really want to be helpful, I think, pack up my apartment and ship my stuff here.

"I'm fucked up," I say eloquently.

Simon is an only child who hasn't lived at home since he was seven. "You're thinking that nothing in my experience corresponds to what you're feeling," he says.

I hate when he does that.

"Maybe," I concede.

"That's not quite true."

"Look, Simon. It's lovely of you to call"—I assume my best British manners—"but it's already late, and there are still things I need to do."

"I won't keep you," says Simon. "But you are on my mind increasingly."

I say nothing.

"I—I guess—I don't—" Simon at a loss for words makes me curl up like an infant.

"I can't stay on," I say miserably. "I'm sorry."

"Who can care for you while you're there? Care? Care about you?" He is stuttering.

This conversation is becoming a minor nightmare. "I have to go. I have to."

"Then I look forward to your arrival," he says formally.

I respond very maturely to this turn of events by crawling beneath the afghan and yanking it over my head.

LAST
DAY

FOURTEEN

"Eve, wake up."

My mother's voice is drilling a hole in my brain.

"Why is it dark?" My own voice is whiny, stretching the word "dark" into two syllables.

"It's six in the morning."

She has my attention. "Aren't you the mother who brought us up to believe there was only one six o'clock in the day?"

"But I haven't had a turn to talk to you." She extends her hands for me to pull myself up.

"Take a ticket," I say, secretly pleased.

"I made coffee."

"Real?"

"Espresso," she announces.

"There is a God," I intone. At the end of shiva, I have my mother to myself as we head to the kitchen.

"What happens next?" she says, looking expectant.

I am afraid to violate our harmony. "How about marriage, children, and a house with a yard? Just like you?"

She has the grace to laugh. "I'm not proposing my life as an example."

"I hope not."

My mother looks chastened. "I know it wasn't easy, what happened with me and your father. I was on a journey—"

"No journey metaphors."

"You're intimidating me."

Duly reprimanded.

"Your father could not listen to me. Although he listens to his clients very carefully," she says. "Now that I'm older, different qualities seem important."

"But Tam's broken your heart."

"Do you think I would give up even one memory of Tam? I can still feel her fuzzy new head against my neck in the middle of the night."

But what about me? I want to add.

"And my recall isn't less just because you were second,"

my mother says serenely. "You were such a peaceful girl, the most beautiful baby in the hospital."

"And smart," I say, out of habit.

"Of course. But don't underestimate beauty. And I'm not referring to Nell."

"Was she as gorgeous as Nana claims?"

"I didn't see her often," my mother says. "Daddy thought she wasn't the greatest influence. And she was always moving around. But when she pulled up in her snazzy car and rang our bell with some tinsel gift I couldn't live without, she was irresistible. You could get drunk just talking to her."

"What must that be like?"

"It was more than physical beauty," my mother clarifies. "She had a spark that made everything fun. Nana was no better at withstanding her than Gil and I, however much she may deny it."

"Or she wouldn't talk about it so much."

"Right," says my mother conclusively. "And you think I'm frivolous, like Nell."

"Not really," I equivocate.

"You do. Your father did, too, in his day, but neither of you understood. The counters—" she says, waving a dampened cloth in my direction.

"'Neither of you understood,'" I prod her, standing up. "About beauty. Then explain." I abandon the counters.

"You think it's just the surface of things," she tells me.

"But I am looking at the deep beauty of the world. Beauty is a gift. You received it. Yes, you did," she says, presuming my dissent. "But it was only given to you to give again."

"I'm losing you."

"Words are so frustrating," says my mother.

"Words are my life," I say theatrically.

"Our physical lives are an echo. We're here to see the beauty beneath. When I can make a beautiful room for my family, when I imagine the way they'll feel in a room I've made for them, that's love. I can't understand why women mourn the loss of their beauty."

"You can't? Tam did."

My mother is absentmindedly stroking my hand. "That was for external reasons—like income. To me, if you've been given beauty, it's a responsibility to make beauty with it. It's like the law of energy: Beauty doesn't die; it just takes different forms. The most important thing is to give it back, to leave the world larger."

"Thank you, Leni Riefenstahl."

My mother will not be incited. "I mean beauty bound to love. Moral beauty. Not carelessly wasted, like Nell's. More like Winifred's."

For a moment I don't catch the reference.

"Your Winifred," she says. "Wasn't she beautiful?"

"Radiant, until the very end."

"Did she ignore it and pretend she wasn't? Or did she put it to good use?" my mother asks shrewdly.

I see Winifred on her first trip to Africa, telling young women at the High School Speech Day to "hold beauty fast," looking herself like a young goddess as she returned to England to take up the cause of racial injustice with all her powers.

My mother the philosopher.

"I am much larger because I was Tam's mother," she says. "Everything she did is still with us. The facts of her beauty. Her children. The life she lived well."

"But you're shattered."

"Of course I'm shattered. This is the week we allow ourselves to be. But I know what I need to do afterward."

"I wish I did. I want to rewind time," I cry. "Go backward. Tam will be alive, and you'll be married to Daddy again."

"We can never, never go back."

"I don't know what happens now," I say childishly.

"You will," my mother says, without the edge in her voice I am accustomed to hearing. "I believe Tam is leaving you gifts all the time. Soon you'll be able to see them."

"Will I know what to do about Simon?" I ask, as if my mother is a fortune-teller.

"And work," she says. "One follows the other, and it doesn't matter which comes first. You need to decide."

"What?"

"Something," she says vaguely.

"Mum, what was it about Nell? Why was Nana so afraid of her?"

"Do you know what she did at the cottage when she was fourteen? Do you know who her first boyfriend was?"

I look inquiring.

"Mrs. Floyd's son," my mother declaims.

"But—"

"That's right," she says. "He wasn't Jewish. Can you imagine? In those years, it's hard to say which family was more horrified. We were good neighbors, but Nell broke the barrier. They had to send her away. And you know? I don't think she was interested in him at all. Not only that: the man is almost ninety, he's been married more than sixty years, and he still asks after her. To this day. I don't have the heart to tell him she died. If you could bottle what she had!"

"She did it her way."

"And left a trail of suffering. That boy got off easy. Every summer I hear again what a sight she was in her white bathing suit, rowing down the river, the talk of the town. So don't be defeated," she says.

"Because Nell looked so good in a bathing suit? Mum, you still believe everything can be remedied."

"I love the way you talk," she says. "'Remedied.' No, I

don't think perfect happiness is possible. I don't even think perfect interior design is possible."

"That's enlightenment."

"But it's noble to try. Imperfection is starting to interest me. I made mistakes," she says proudly.

"They were costly," I say. "You hurt us so much. We could have been a regular family."

"Do you think that if your father and I had stayed together, Tam wouldn't have died?"

"Maybe," I say sullenly.

"Eve," she admonishes me.

"I can wish, can't I?"

"And you think that's why you haven't married? But Tam married wonderfully well."

I am manifestly silent.

"Surely you're not jealous of Tam? Not now."

"I am definitely not jealous of Tam," I tell her. "Not now, and—believe it or not—not ever. Except, maybe, for the kids."

She brightens. "That's good news."

"Not yet," I warn her.

"Two grandchildren are not enough for me," my mother says. "And don't think I'm saying this just because I'm an old-fashioned woman who never had a real job, as you liked to notify me when you were a teenager. There isn't a mother who doesn't worry, full-time, about why her unmarried children aren't married and having children themselves."

"Really?"

"It's all my friends talk about—even the most feminist."

"If you remarry Daddy, I'll marry Simon."

"Tam liked him a lot," my mother says. "She said he was a man of virtue."

"Simon?"

"Yes, she thought he was good. Upright. That was Tam's highest compliment."

"It's not how I think of him." Or her.

"Why, is he bad?" she says with amusement.

"You know I like them a little bit bad."

"Everyone needs some spice. I did."

"I don't want to know."

"And I wouldn't tell you. But those days are long ago. Don't be defeated," my mother says again.

"Why not?"

"Because you don't know what will happen next. You always wanted to."

"What?"

"Know," says my mother.

◆

Nana's vigorous footsteps invade the front hall.

"Come on, Nana," I inveigle her as soon as she walks in. "Hang out with me."

She deigns to sit.

"What would revive us?" I ask her. "Tea?"

I make hers medium dark, pouring it exactly four minutes into steeping.

She loops her finger into the handle. "Do you still like yours so black?"

I'm surprised she remembers. "I haven't changed. In the little ways."

"Nor in the big ones," she says.

"At least I'm consistent." I am trying to retrieve my provocation for old time's sake.

"Yes," Nana states, "you were always boy crazy." Her jaw, as she raises her head to look at me, is pugnacious.

I cannot decide if I should sacrifice myself in order to restore her.

"You," she says, "still remind me of someone."

Sandy's visitation marks the end of all restraint. "I'm nothing like your sister. Did I ever steal Tam's boyfriends?" Au contraire. "Did I borrow her wedding clothes and ruin them? You're the one who's boy crazy," I say wildly. "You've always liked boys better than girls. You probably wished I were a boy when I was born."

I expect Nana to deride me. When she doesn't, a purity of terror descends upon me.

She looks down at her tea.

As always, I feel the need to be outspoken before her composure. "I know you've had the natural sorrows," I tell her, thinking of Grandpa and of her first love. "But this death is the first—"

"No, it's not," she says shortly.

I find the discipline to match her reserve with my own.

Each of us is waiting for the other, as if we have been engaged in the most courteous of conversations. Nana's posture is again unbending. And yet she would not allow herself this idleness if she did not want to speak.

"Is the tea strong?" I say inanely. She shakes her head, then nods, another portent.

"Nell used to have an expression," Nana tells me. "She never drank liquor: 'I've spirit enough without it,' she would say. But whenever she had a problem—and Lord knows she had her share—she would pour herself a cup of tea and decree, 'A little brandy for the old girl.' I wish I could tell you it set her straight."

I carry my own cup to the table and, as I have done all my life, wait until Nana is ready.

"I never thought he was right," Nana says quietly.

Laurie? I ask myself, but she continues.

"They didn't believe me. In those years, doctors were gods, and mothers—women—were just to be tolerated. I'm not an intuitive person," she tells me unnecessarily, "but I was a scientist, trained as an observer. I knew something was the matter."

Since my childhood I have longed for Nana to tell me a secret, about the romance of her youth, about her flapper heyday. But I understand from my clenched body that what is about to transpire will not be some overdue girlish confidence.

"It's been fifty-seven years," she says, "and I think about that tiny boy every day."

My mother is sixty; my uncle fifty.

"When the doctor said, 'I want to send him for tests,' I started praying. I prayed with all my heart. And when he died—"

My own heart collides with my ribs.

"—it took the starch out of me. They wouldn't let me sit shiva—the baby was too young—but I sat, believe me. And I made people come to see me. When I got up, I was a different woman. Before, I had known suffering as a cause, abstractly, for other people. Now I knew it stamped in my flesh."

She hesitates. I am afraid she will unravel and that I will not know how to comfort her.

"If it weren't for your grandfather—" Her chin is high.

"What did he do?" I am walking across the kitchen mechanically, counting floor tiles—one, two, three and a half.

"'Don't pray for a different ending,' Grandpa said. 'Pray for the strength to bear what we were given.'"

"Hard," I tell her.

"Truthful. Everyone else was reassuring. 'Don't worry, you'll have other children.' But I didn't want other children. I wanted only him. For a long, long time I refused to think about another. That was the prescription in those days, to get pregnant right away, as if nothing had happened."

Nana cannot stop talking.

"Thank goodness your grandfather was patient. I threw myself into my work—and made a lot of progress, I must say. It took me nearly ten years to be ready again. At thirty-nine, I was considered a medical hazard, but I paid them no mind. Did I ever tell you," she resumes the impassive tone I know, "that before the war, pregnant women would go outside only after dark?"

She allows me to take her papery hand, which I do not relinquish. My mother pushes open the door, looks at Nana's face, at mine, and withdraws. My father, seconds later, mimics her. Behind the closed door they speak in muted voices, intimate syllables I cannot decipher.

Nana follows my gaze. "They have a lot to talk about now," she says.

"I hope they don't fight." I revert to another era. "It's a good thing they're divorced. I hear the death of a child can really break up a marriage."

"Not always," Nana says.

"I'm a jerk," I say instantly. "A tactless jerk."

"Sometimes," Nana says, taking no notice of me, "sorrow is even more binding than joy."

My mother, entering a second time with Gil and my father behind her, looks like the proverbial cat that swallowed the canary. "Glad it's over?" I interpret her face.

"Yes and no," she says.

"Is it me, or is everyone a little strange this morning? Not you, Nana," I backpedal.

"Maybe we see that it's time to get on with our lives," says my mother.

I am mystified.

"Are you ready to go back?" Gil asks.

"I haven't thought about it. But I'm sure it will be odd."

"Will Simon meet you at the airport?" says my father.

My mother glances at him and then looks down demurely. I would love to believe she is hinting to him about not pressuring me, but subtlety is not in her lexicon.

"We never meet each other at airports."

"Reunions can be nice," Gil says.

"I guess so." I sound dubious.

"They haven't had that kind of relationship," my mother pronounces.

"What kind?" Nana asks.

"Romantic. It's been more—"

I listen, bemused, for her explanation.

"—practical," my mother concludes. "Grown-up."

"Grown-up can't be romantic?" my father says.

Who is going to change the subject?

"Croissants anyone?" my mother asks cheerfully.

We all laugh. "Croissants," I say, "are very romantic."

We are clearing our plates when the doorbell rings.

"Why don't you get it, Eve?" says my mother.

I am immediately suspicious. There is something overly knowing in her tone that I do not like. A premonition about Laurie gives me pause, my hand on the knob. Surely he would not be complicit in my mother's unwitting plot of a grand farewell.

Like an elderly woman who lives alone, I lift the batik to look through the etched pane in the front door.

There, his earnest face looking back at my shocked one, is Simon.

FIFTEEN

AND SO IT COMES TO PASS THAT INSTEAD OF A ROUND in my old neighborhood with my family of origin, I am pacing the subdued morning street with Simon. My mother and my father, arm in arm and no doubt agog, are behind me, with Ben and Gil bringing up the rear.

Simon and I have already fought about the drama of his showing up, uninvited, "like some stupid Mr. Darcy," I contend.

He is uncustomarily speechless in response to that charge.

"You'll never understand," I tell him.

"Why not?" he says reasonably, keeping up with my vicious stride.

"Because now I'm an only child."

"What do you think I am?" he says.

"You never had siblings. You didn't undergo a change of status."

Simon looks behind him as if someone is stalking him, a tendency I realize is characteristic.

"We're in the heart of residential Toronto," I say. "Who do you think is tracking you, except members of my prying family?"

"Old habit," says Simon.

We walk together. I have to admit: it is unexpectedly consoling to have him here. I point to a corner thick with trees. "That's where I hid behind the car, and my parents thought I was dead."

"But I did," he says.

"Did what?" I take his hand to guide him across the street.

"Did undergo a change of status," he explains. "Before I was born."

"Your mother had a miscarriage?" I say, disoriented. "You were one of twins?"

"I am"—he stands still—"the fifth child of my parents, and the only one alive."

"Metaphorically?"

"Literally," he says, as though I have called him a liar. "My father lost a daughter and a son, and my mother lost two children; I don't know what kind."

"Lost?" I say idiotically.

"Lost, you North American. The war."

I have to sit on the curb. Since I am holding his hand, now gripped in mine so unrelentingly he cannot loose it, he is bent over me awkwardly.

"You okay?" a woman calls out from the open window of her car with un-Canadian nosiness.

I wave her off with a gesture I hope looks normal.

Simon sits down beside me. "I'm sorry. I didn't mean to tell you like that. In fact," he seems surprised, "I didn't mean to tell you at all."

"Ever?" I say, surprised in turn. "It's quite a fact to withhold."

"I don't talk about it," he says. "My parents never told me."

I pose the obvious question.

"I found a snapshot in his wallet. I wasn't looking for it," he defends himself.

"I'm not judging."

"I asked my mother, and she told me about my father."

"But not about herself?"

Simon shook his head. I am astonished to see his tears.

"We don't have to talk about it, either."

"I don't know much more. Every night I heard my father screaming. I thought everyone's father called out German names while he was sleeping: 'Valter.' 'Dora.'"

I look at him—his narrow, nervy face, his dark eyes brimming beneath his tweed cap. If he threw up his hands, he'd look like that little boy in the Warsaw Ghetto.

"Aren't you supposed to circle the block?" Simon asks me.

"I think so, but I can't remember why."

"You're returning to life," says Simon. "Going back into the world after staying in the house for seven days."

"I can't escape," I cry out. "I can't bring her back."

"Tam?"

"Winifred," I say. "She died too young, and even when I get my degree she'll still be dead."

"Undeniably true. Which means you might as well finish."

The eros of renunciation: Surrender that, too?

Simon's incisive face is beautiful.

"All right," I say, as if he is forcing me. "I will. Must everything be so complicated?"

Not a word.

"And why is your silence so alarming? Can't you pretend you're a regular person?"

"Let me think."

I groan.

"Okay, I've finished thinking. You'll never hear a more straightforward sentence than this one," Simon declares.

"Try me."

"Eve," he says. "Will you marry me?"

Look who is mute now.

Decades ago, Nana rests in the shade of the cottage porch, and this is what she sees: Her sister, Nell, standing at the well in brilliant sun, the grass beneath her bare feet glittering with water as she pumps coil after glassy coil into the pail. Nell's arms flash as she raises the handle of the pump and draws it down.

Across from her is a young man, a man who is wooing Nana. While Nana watches, Nell anoints him from the glinting pail. He flicks drops from his forehead, from his cheeks.

Nell is laughing as she cups her hands. The water she tosses at him falls from his hair in jeweled beads.

He looks bewildered.

Nell's hair has loosened, shining copper strands falling

about her shoulders. Her white dress is beginning to grow translucent. Already, the bodice is plastered to her skin. Her slip straps emerge from the thin fabric, and then they, too, dissolve. Nana, squinting, can see symmetrical dots of rose beneath Nell's chemise.

Then Nell's liquid skirts part at the thighs. In glorious midsummer, the dress has turned to flesh. Nana, her face pressed against the screen, contemplates the shadowy heart at the place where her sister's legs meet.

Nell picks up the pail and, disregarding the young man's protests, dances toward him. As she runs, shimmering wings of water dash from the pail's lip. On the emerald lawn she appears naked, triumphant, leaping hair and gold skin, and the darkening triangle, explicit, magnet of Nana's attention.

The young man peers at Nell as she lifts her chin to the heavens. Then she looks at him directly, her profile outlined in light, mouth softening.

Nana is motionless as he thinks. Then, slowly, he clasps Nell's wrists and raises her arms, crossing them back against her chest in an X of supplication.

As the man who will become my grandfather walks with resolution toward the house, Nana observes his deliberate gait, step by considered step away from her sister, and decides.

"Yes?" says Simon.

We have completed the circle and are at the front door.

"No?" he adds, reluctantly.

"Maybe." Decode that, smarty-pants. "When I finish my dissertation, I may as well."

He looks at me and cannot help laughing. "I'll take that as a yes," he says.

◆

Having nothing, yet possessing all things: Winifred was given her source and revelation.

My mother, who must have passed me on the way home while I was staring at Simon in stupefaction, is at the door the instant she hears my key.

I do not even wait to take off my coat. "You knew he was coming," I accuse her.

"Naturally," she says.

My mother hugs Simon and motions toward the living room, looking smug. Immediately, my uncle presents himself. "There you are," he says to my mother. "And you," he turns to me.

"And you?" He walks up to Simon, who holds out his hand in introduction.

My uncle can scarcely contain himself. My father is next, with Ben on his heels.

"Meet the family," I say to Simon.

"He just happened to drop by," I tell them helpfully. "Do you want to interrogate him now or later?"

Simon shakes one offered hand after another. "My intentions are honorable," he says. "Where's your grandmother?"

I dare not leave him alone with my blood relatives. "Who is going to find Nana?"

"I will," says Gil, with mischief in his eyes.

"They're all I have," I say to Simon.

And here is Nana, perfectly coiffed and turned out, as usual.

"Delighted to meet you," says Simon.

Nana chooses one of her chilling glances, but he merely looks amused.

Simon is not afraid of Nana, I inform Tam.

While I'm talking to my sister, Nana and Simon embark on an animated conversation about advances in organic chemistry, yet another subject about which he seems to know an inordinate amount. They are sitting side by side on the couch, chatting away incomprehensibly.

I see how it is. Death is the ultimate choosing: This, not that. Him, not her.

He is winning her over, I tell Tam.

To which she replies from beyond: "I told you so."

© Eugene Weisberg

NESSA RAPOPORT was born in Toronto, Canada. She is the author of a novel, *Preparing for Sabbath*, and a collection of prose poems, *A Woman's Book of Grieving*. Her memoir, *House on the River*, was awarded a grant by the Canada Council for the Arts. Her essays and reviews have appeared in *The New York Times* and the *Los Angeles Times*, among other publications. She lives in New York with her husband, artist Tobi Kahn.